"Stress and na... mix well."

CW00363064

"Afraid I'm going to ... Macy asked softly. Th... outside, lighting the tower room in a dim peach glow like candlelight.

"I'm afraid you won't have to," he answered honestly.

His life was coming apart at the seams. How easy it would be to forget his troubles in her.

She deserved better.

Clint faced her and couldn't resist tucking a strand of dark, wavy hair behind her ear while she studied him with luminous eyes.

"I don't want to hurt you," he breathed.

"I don't want to be hurt. But I would like to be held."

She let him decide. He liked that about her. It wouldn't have taken much to push him over the edge. A kiss. A touch. But she stood back and let him decide.

In the end, she didn't have to push him over the edge.

He leaped willingly.

Available in October 2006 from Silhouette Sensation

Her Last Defence
VICKIE TAYLOR

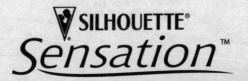

SILHOUETTE®
Sensation™

DID YOU PURCHASE THIS BOOK WITHOUT A COVER?
If you did, you should be aware it is **stolen property** as it was
reported *unsold and destroyed* by a retailer. Neither the author nor
the publisher has received any payment for this book.

*All the characters in this book have no existence outside the
imagination of the author, and have no relation whatsoever to anyone
bearing the same name or names. They are not even distantly inspired
by any individual known or unknown to the author, and all the
incidents are pure invention.*

*All Rights Reserved including the right of reproduction in whole or
in part in any form. This edition is published by arrangement with
Harlequin Enterprises II B.V. The text of this publication or any part
thereof may not be reproduced or transmitted in any form or by any
means, electronic or mechanical, including photocopying, recording,
storage in an information retrieval system, or otherwise, without the
written permission of the publisher.*

*This book is sold subject to the condition that it shall not, by way of
trade or otherwise, be lent, resold, hired out or otherwise circulated
without the prior consent of the publisher in any form of binding or
cover other than that in which it is published and without a similar
condition including this condition being imposed on the subsequent
purchaser.*

*Silhouette, Silhouette Sensation and Colophon are registered
trademarks of Harlequin Books S.A., used under licence.*

*First published in Great Britain 2006
Silhouette Books, Eton House, 18-24 Paradise Road,
Richmond, Surrey TW9 1SR*

© Vickie Spears 2005

*ISBN-13: 978 0 373 27451 2
ISBN-10: 0 373 27451 3*

18-1006

*Printed and bound in Spain
by Litografia Rosés S.A., Barcelona*

VICKIE TAYLOR

has always loved books—the way they look, the way they feel and most especially the way the stories inside them bring whole new worlds to life. She views her recent transition from reading to writing books as a natural extension of this longtime love. Vickie lives in Aubrey, Texas, a small town dubbed "The Heart of Horse Country," where, in addition to writing romance novels, she raises American Quarter Horses and volunteers her time to help homeless and abandoned animals. Vickie loves to hear from readers. Write to her at: PO Box 633, Aubrey, TX 76227, USA.

Chapter 1

It was a perfect night in hell.

Autumn leaves flickered silver and gold under a harvest moon. The surface of Lake Farrell, the best fishing hole in southeast Texas, rippled like black velvet. And the air, sharp with the scent of pine, was clean enough to scrub a month's worth of city smog out of a man's lungs with each breath.

Once, Texas Ranger Sergeant Clint Hayes had thought the old fishing cabin his Grandpop Charlie had left him was the closest place to heaven on earth. But not any longer. Not since a pair of beady eyes and a sallow smile had begun their nightly torment from the pier where Grandpop's old dinghy still bobbed on the swells.

Sitting in a weathered grapevine chair on the stoop of the cabin, his bare feet propped on the porch rail,

Clint narrowed his eyes and stared into the darkness, the soul of the night. "All right, you son of a bitch. This is it."

Only the silence answered. His gut cramped. The Glock .9-millimeter weighed heavily in his right hand. He took a moment to dry his fingers on his jeans, then jerked up the pistol and squeezed off three rounds.

The pale, yellow eyes of his personal demon never wavered.

Jaw clenched and a growl emanating from between his teeth, Clint emptied the clip in one long burst, then threw the gun at the hellish eyes, howling hopelessly because he knew it didn't matter that his bullets hadn't connected. The real monster wasn't out there.

It was inside him.

Breathing hard, he stared at his right hand. Even as he watched, his fingers betrayed him, trembling beyond his control. Finally, he clenched his shaking fist, swallowed hard and accepted the inevitable.

He couldn't hold a gun steady any longer, and a cop who couldn't hit what he aimed at didn't belong on the street.

His career was over.

The deep quiet of the night pressed in on him. Even the nocturnal critters that usually scuttled around the cabin in the wee hours were still, scared off by the gunfire.

An ache so deep it vibrated in his marrow pushed him to his feet and off the porch, over the carpet of pine needles toward the lake, where the yellow smiley face he'd painted on a beer bottle and set on a piling as a target goaded him in the waning moonlight.

"You win, damn it!" he yelled as he swiped at the bottle with his foot. "Are you happy now?"

Pain exploded up his leg as flesh and bone connected with glass and sent the bottle arcing over the water. He hopped and cursed, rubbing the sore spot.

Well, at least *some* of his nerves still worked right.

Hobbling back ashore, he allowed himself a single sardonic laugh. 'Cool-hand Clint' people called him. Wasn't so cool now, was he?

Fresh out of good curses, he turned his eyes to the black canopy overhead. He wasn't a Ranger anymore. Couldn't be. And without the job to ground him, he felt like a spacewalking astronaut who'd come untethered from his ship. Weightless. Rudderless. Drifting in the vast vacuum of space.

And very, very alone.

Searching for answers in the sky, he tried to focus on the points of light, the stars, not the boundless black void between them. Sailors used to navigate by the stars, he knew, but no matter how long he stared at them, how hard he concentrated, the chips of cold light charted no course for him.

Sighing, he turned to head back to the cabin when a flash over his right shoulder stopped him. The light flared blue for a moment, then flamed into an orange streak. A shooting star, he thought at first, then realized it couldn't be. It was too bright and too close, moving too slowly.

An airplane, he realized a second later. And in trouble, by the sound of it. Its engine sputtered and whined as it passed overhead so low that Clint ducked reflexively. He just made out the shape of a small jet—blink-

ing wing lights, oval windows in the fuselage, a flash
of the white tail—before he lost sight of the aircraft behind the trees.

His breath stalled in his chest as he waited, listening.

The crash, when it came, wasn't the booming explosion he expected. It sounded more like a distant car
wreck. Metal screeched. Wood groaned and splintered.
The air seemed to shudder around him. By the time silence had reclaimed the night, a pale glow, like a false
sunrise, lit the treetops where the plane had gone down.
Clint studied the fire, gauging its distance and how long
it would take him to get there.

Tomorrow he would have to call the Ranger office
and tell them the truth. Tell them he could no longer be
the only thing he'd ever wanted to be.

But tonight, he was still a Texas Ranger.

From Macy Attois's vantage point in a helicopter hovering above the wreckage, the tail of the aircraft jutting
out of the east Texas thicket looked like the rear fin of a
whale about to plunge beneath the ocean's surface. But
the scorched earth and shattered tree limbs around the
crash site left no doubt that airplanes were not supposed
to plunge. Or that when they did, it usually ended badly.

One white wing weighed down the boughs of a thick
spruce. Bits of plastic and cloth, chunks of smoldering
metal freckled the brambles along a trail of devastation
hundreds of yards long. Emergency workers in reflective vests and hard hats picked through the debris, one
spreading a white sheet over a hunk of fuselage that
looked as though it might once have been a cockpit.

Tears filled Macy's eyes as a firefighter stabbed a red flag—the indicator for the location of human remains—into the ground at one corner of the sheet. A thin plume of smoke curled upward from the spot as if to mark the trail of a soul leaving its earthly existence. Overhead a half dozen buzzards circled, hoping for a chance at the body left behind.

Grief rolled heavily in Macy's chest. God, how many dead? Two in the cockpit. Then there was Jeffries, the man who'd been hired to tend the cargo. Cory Holcomb, the lab tech. Timlen Zufria, the Malaysian doctor working with them.

And David.

A strand of long, brown hair broke free from Macy's braid to lash against her cheek. She turned her head away from the open door of the chopper as it banked low over the remnants of the once-sleek aircraft, scattering the buzzards.

Oh, David.

Closing her eyes, she choked back tears. She would not cry. Not in front of the others. Not when there was work to do.

How many times had David told her there was no room for emotion in medical research?

She'd never become as astute as him at separating her feelings from the job. Those feelings were the reason she'd become a doctor. She *cared* about people.

She'd cared about David.

"This is as close as I can get you," the pilot's voice crackled in her headset.

She opened her eyes, noting thankfully that they'd

passed over the broken ruins of the jet. Below them now lay only a patchy gray-brown blanket of scrub mesquite west of the debris field. To the east the midmorning sun broke free of a cloud and flared brightly enough to burn Macy's already-stinging eyes.

Squinting as she swept her gaze over the clearing, to the seemingly endless woods all around it, Macy gave the pilot a shaky thumbs-up. "It'll do."

At least the plane hadn't crashed in a populated area. The souls aboard the chartered jet were gone, but there was still a chance a larger disaster could be averted.

As the Bell 429 descended, she hung her headset on the peg behind her seat and put on her helmet, careful to seal the double cuff between it and the neck of her environmental suit securely. The four other members of the team took her cue and donned their gear. She checked the airtight closure on each person's wrists and ankles before they climbed out of the helicopter.

"Remember." Her respirator muffled the words. She raised her voice to make sure no one missed her point. "These suits may be the only thing standing between life and death out there. *Your* life and *your* death. Make sure you take care of them."

Maybe Macy was being overly cautious, but at least worrying about her people distracted her from thinking about what lay ahead. Twisted metal. Twisted bodies. Her and David's research—work that might have saved so many lives—gone up in smoke. Or maybe down in flames was a better analogy.

The research was inconsequential now. There would

be no laboratory-controlled experiments. No computer-modeled projections.

No containment, if her worst fears proved true.

Curtis Leahy, the logistics officer with surfer-dude good looks and the shaggy blond hair to match, nodded. "We all know the risks."

Sweat trickled into Macy's eye. Texas was still warm in early October, and her anxiety wasn't helping. Unable to wipe the perspiration away because of her face shield, she blinked the droplets out of her eyes. "Then let's none of us become statistics, okay?"

Noting that Susan and Christian Fargier, the twin brother and sister lab techs who'd brought excellent references to the CDC from the Mayo clinic in Minnesota, wore properly concerned expressions, Macy led her people toward the wreckage and prayed they weren't too late to stop a tragedy from becoming a catastrophe.

One by one, the firefighters, sheriff's deputies and forestry-service employees working around the wreck turned toward Macy and her team. They leaned on rakes and shovels, their faces smudged with ash, eyes watery and red. Sweat plastered their clothes to their bodies, rolled from beneath the headbands of their hard hats. They stared at the crew walking toward them as if Macy and her team were Martians emerging from a flying saucer.

Which is exactly what they looked like, Macy supposed, with their orange biohazard suits and respirator packs, carrying medical supplies in dimpled silver suitcases that caught the sunlight in bright flashes.

Macy fumbled with the pouch at her waist, pulled out

her ID and held it up in a gloved hand. "I'm Dr. Macy Attois with the Centers for Disease Control in Atlanta."

The workers' eyes turned wary. Several dropped the tools they'd been carrying. A few began to back away.

Macy's heart rate kicked up a notch. She worked to keep her voice steady. Her panic would only feed theirs.

"This site is a biohazard," she continued as unemotionally as she could manage. Some of them looked so young….

"Biohazard?" a Boy-Scout-faced young man in a brown forestry service shirt asked, the whites of his eyes standing out against flushed cheeks.

The crowd rumbled behind him. "What the—?"

"Did she say bio—"

"Hellfire—"

Macy raised her voice to an officious tone. "For your own safety, it's important that you move away from the wreckage. My team will set up a triage area and check everyone out." She heard the latches on the portable suitcases snick open as Susan and Christian set up behind her.

"Triage, hell." A wild-eyed young sheriff's deputy with a mustache that looked like a horseshoe hung upside down on his upper lip edged away from the others. His hand gripped the butt of the pistol on his hip. "I'm getting out of here."

"That's the worst thing you could do," Macy said. She didn't add that the state troopers already setting up roadblocks outside the Sabine National Forest, where the jet had crashed, had been ordered to turn back anyone who tried to leave the area—with lethal force, if necessary. "If you've been exposed, you need specialized treatment."

The deputy swayed as if unsure whether or not to make a run for it. A man in a sooty, blue-flannel shirt caught him by the epaulet.

"Exposed to what?" the man asked.

Macy's first impression of him was *rugged.* He wore a tan that couldn't be bought in a salon. His body was long and lean, not overly muscled, and yet exuding a sense of sinewy strength, like a high-tension steel cable. When he moved through the crowd, pulling the deputy with him, the workers parted like the waters before Moses to give him room.

Whoever he was, he commanded the respect of the locals.

She waited until he'd almost reached her before answering his question with one of her own. "Who am I speaking to?"

His hair was brown, tempered by shades of gray that might have been natural or might have been a dusting of ash from the fire. His cheeks were thin, not an ounce of extra flesh on them. His nose looked as if it might have been broken a time or two and his mouth slashed across his face in a stiff line that said he didn't smile much. But most notable were his eyes, deep-set, with rims bloodshot from the smoke around irises so gray they appeared metallic. And completely unreadable.

And calm as the Dead Sea.

She shook herself mentally, ignoring the shiver his stare sent crawling down her spine. She would not be intimidated by dead-calm eyes. Calm was good. They could all use a little calm right now.

"You'd be speaking to Sergeant Clint Hayes, ma'am," he answered. "Texas Rangers."

Macy's eyes widened. No wonder he commanded the respect of the locals. The Texas Rangers walked on water in this part of the country.

Hope made her heartbeat flutter. Hope, and those unearthly eyes he had fixed on her. Surely with his help, she could get this crowd to cooperate. How did the old saying go? *One riot, one ranger?*

"Sergeant, why don't you gather your crew," she said softly, calling on his leadership. "Help me get them lined up over by my assistants. Then I'll explain everything to you."

He glanced over his shoulder at the assembly murmuring behind him, then turned to her, his straight lips pressed thin. "Why don't you explain everything right here. To all of us."

She tried to warn him off with a look, but his steely gaze knocked hers away as easily as a master swordsman parrying the thrust of an inferior opponent. A flush she couldn't blame on the confinement of the bio suit heated her cheeks, but she lifted her chin, nonetheless. She had a job to do. Lives depended on her doing it.

"This plane was bound for the CDC research facility in Atlanta." Her heart thundered with an urgency she hoped didn't carry into her voice. "It was carrying a contagion."

"What kind of contagion?"

She hesitated. "The flight originated in Malaysia."

"ARFIS," one of the workers behind him said, fear riding high in his voice.

She nodded, grateful for the protective shield on her helmet that would hide her reaction to the statement. "Acute Respiratory Failure Infectious Syndrome. If containment has been breached…"

Tears welled up as the image of the mass graves required simply to keep up with burial needs in Malaysia, where the disease had originated, sprang to mind unbidden.

Among the workers, only the Ranger looked unaffected.

"Then we're all dead," he said, his voice as unmoved as his eyes.

Chapter 2

Outrage swirled in Clint's chest like a cyclone, circling ever tighter and faster until it spun itself into a hard knot that sat on the floor of his stomach where it could be kicked aside like a pebble on a sidewalk. Nothing of what he felt showed on his face—he made sure of it.

After six-and-a-half hours of shoveling dirt over the smoldering remains of the airplane, suppressing a wildfire that could have consumed thousands of acres of trees and wildlife, Clint's bad arm ached like a son of a bitch. The smoke had burned his nose and throat raw. His eyes were watering like he'd been hit square in the face with a shot of Mace. But they'd saved the Sabine National Forest, him and the others who had worked through the dark and then dawn, so they weren't complaining.

Until Typhoid Mary showed up and told them they might have traded their lives for it.

"ARFIS?" Clint nearly spat the word. "What in God's name were you thinking, bringing that bug here?"

The woman squared her shoulders. At least he thought she squared her shoulders. It was hard to tell with her wearing that astronaut suit.

"I was thinking I might develop a vaccine."

He narrowed his eyes. Oh, yeah. She'd squared off, all right.

She took a step forward, a chess piece moved to block his advance. Her respirator rasped with each breath, making her sound like some kind of neon Darth Vader. "I was thinking I might save a few million lives."

"Playing God."

"Playing doctor," the woman spat right back at him. She took another step forward. The glare on her face shield dimmed and Clint got his first real look at her—and that pebble he'd discounted so easily a moment ago slammed back into his gut like a boulder tumbling downhill. She might not be too big, or too smart, playing with bugs like ARFIS, but she had a face that would inspire a horde of Huns to sing like angels.

A hint of wild, dark hair framed her heart-shaped face. Her mouth pursed into a perfect bow, her lips naturally rosy. Her skin tone was olive and her nose turned up just enough at the end to give the face personality. She was alluring, exotic and his body tightened against his will.

He tried to stop the physical reaction without success, then tried to ignore it and failed almost as miserably.

What was wrong with him? Women did not affect him this way. Ever.

"It's what I do," she finished, though he hardly heard her past his clamoring pulse.

She stepped past him to face the gathered workers. "Let's not get ahead of ourselves," she told them. The raspy respirator only made her French-Cajun accent sultrier. Sexier. "We don't know that the virus has escaped the containers it was packed in, yet, much less whether any of you have been exposed to it. There's no reason to panic."

She was good, Clint gave her that. Had a nice soothing way about her that sounded like she really cared. But the workers were beyond soothing. As his hormones cooled, Clint could feel the tension mounting behind him, fear rising.

"If it's so safe here," someone called out. "Then why are y'all wearing them spacesuits?"

"The suits are just a precaution. I'm sure you can understand—"

"I understand that *we* ain't got no suits."

A wave of murmured "Yeahs" rippled through the crowd. Their growing restlessness had the hairs prickling on the back of Clint's neck. Trouble was brewing. The lady was in over her head. She didn't know these people. Didn't understand that they weren't city folk, conditioned to expect the unexpected. They lived a quiet, routine life. The possibility of being at the epicenter of an epidemic was going to scare the hell out of them. And fear could make people do crazy things.

"I seen those people on TV," Deputy Sheriff Slick

Burgress spoke up, finger-combing his long mustache anxiously. "The sick ones in Malaysia. They drowned in their own blood."

"Those were extreme cases—"

"Then you admit it could happen!" someone shouted.

"People, please. Even if the virus did escape, it can only live in the air for three, maybe four minutes. Once it settles from the air it can only survive if it lands in some sort of moisture, oil- or water-based. You'd have to touch it—"

"Lady we've been climbing over this wreck since before dawn putting out fires. There's hydraulic oil and fuel and water all over the place, and we done touched every bit of it," Cal Jenkins, an EMT from Hempaxe, the closest town, admitted. His voice rose, shook. "I got a wife. Kids."

"The best thing you can do for them is allow my team to examine you."

"Screw that. I'm gettin' out of here." He threw his shovel down.

"Me, too."

"I'm with you. She can't stop us."

"That's the worst thing you can do," the woman cried.

Out of the corner of his eye, Clint saw some of the workers edge away. The fear in the air was palpable, and ready to combust.

Damn.

He didn't like the way she'd sauntered in here, safe behind her protective face shield and airtight suit, and told two-dozen men they might have contracted a fatal illness. He didn't like that she asked them to line up to be poked and prodded before they'd had time to absorb the information and he especially didn't like the way his heart dropped between his legs just from looking at her.

Stiffly, careful to keep his gaze on the crowd and not her, he clenched his free hand into a fist in an uncharacteristic display of frustration and turned to stand shoulder to shoulder with her, dragging the deputy along with him. He didn't like taking her side against his own folk, but until he actually turned in his gun and badge, he was still a Texas Ranger. He had an obligation.

"She's right." Clint met each worker's gaze, one by one. He stopped the deserters in their tracks with a hard look.

"You standin' against us, Hayes?" a gray-haired firefighter in threadbare turnout gear asked.

"I'm not standing against anybody," he answered carefully, setting his face in the mask of composure that had served him well in situations even more volatile than this one.

Skip Hollister, the pot-bellied mechanic and captain of the volunteer fire department, spat and wiped his face with his arm, leaving a black smear across his pudgy cheek. "If you're not standing with us, then you're against us."

"I'm just saying maybe you ought to think a minute before you go rushing off." And just to make it clear that wasn't a request, he moved his hand to his hip, purposely drawing attention to the bulge of his gun under the untucked tail of his shirt. Habit had made him clip the holster to his belt when he'd rushed out of the cabin before dawn, even though the weapon was useless to him now.

"What are you going to do, shoot me?" Hollister inched away from the crowd. His fingers tightened around the shovel he carried until his knuckles went white.

"I hope I don't have to." Especially since he doubted he could hit the broad side of a barn at more than ten paces.

"I was friends with your grandpop for fifty years, known you all your life. I remember the first time he brought you out fishin' with us. You were just knee-high to a tadpole."

Clint set his mouth in a grim line. "I've grown some since then."

Skip's jaw gaped. "Charlie would roll over in his grave if he saw this. You standing with her agint' your own people."

"Lemme go. I'm gettin' out of here." The deputy still in Clint's grasp squirmed.

Clint turned his attention to him. "Where you going to go, Slick? Home to that wife and kid you're so worried about so you can get them sick, too?"

Slick's gaze fell to his feet.

"What about you, Vern? You got family?" he asked a heavyset paramedic who looked like a rabbit looking for a bolt-hole.

"Mom," the man mumbled. "And a sister."

"You plannin' to carry this disease home to them?"

Vern raised his chin. Resolve mingled with the fear in his eyes. "No, sir!"

"What about the rest of you? You going to march into town, shake hands with your neighbors, pinch their babies' cheeks? You going to be the one to wipe out Hempaxe and a hundred more small towns just like it?"

Clint picked on the deputy because he knew he'd get the answer he wanted. He fisted his hand in the front of the young man's shirt, forcing him to raise his gaze to Clint's. "You going to be the one to start the epidemic, Slick?"

"No, sir!" The deputy's lip curled on the emphatic *sir.*

Clint released his hold on the man's shirt and looked to the man next to him. "What about you, Skip?"

Skip kicked up a clod of dirt with his toe. "Hell, no."

He swept his gaze over the others. "Right now, *if* this thing is out, at least it's contained. There's two thousand acres of forest between civilization and the virus. Are we gonna make sure it stays that way?"

The rumble of yeses and yessirs started slow and quiet, but gained momentum quickly. One by one the workers' chins came up. Their sooty faces were somber, their eyes still scared, but tempered with resignation.

"All right, then. Why don't we all listen to what the lady has to say?" He turned to Dr. Attois. His stomach flipped as their gazes sparked like jumper cables when they touched briefly. The little furrow between her perfectly arched eyebrows drew far too much of his attention. Never mind her tongue flicking out to moisten her lips before she spoke.

Damn. He tightened the screws down on his libido, his expression unmoving. Whatever he saw in her, it wouldn't reach his face. He hoped.

She cleared her throat and looked away. "Symptoms of the virus usually begin to appear within twenty-four hours of exposure, but we can confirm or deny the presence of the virus in your systems after twelve with a simple blood test. We'll move away from the crash site. The first step is for my team to set up the portable decontamination showers and get everyone disinfected. We have choppers coming in from Houston with everything we'll need after that—tents, cots, tables, food. You think of something you need, let me know. I'll get it."

A thin, black-haired young man in turnout gear raised his hand. "Only one thing I need, lady. That's a pencil and some paper."

Heads turned in question toward the man.

"Wife's been after me for years to write out a will," he said. "Guess it's 'bout time I obliged."

At least the workers had settled, thanks to the Ranger. Macy felt sorry for them, knowing the anxiety and the ordeal they faced if ARFIS had indeed escaped, but she had to put that out of her mind. She had a job to do.

A virus to hunt.

She left the men, including Ranger Hayes-with-the-disturbing-eyes, in the competent hands of her team. Susan already had them lining up for interviews and baseline health screenings while Christian and Curtis erected the decon showers that had arrived on the first supply chopper.

"Who was first on scene? Are they still here?" Susan asked. In spite of the rising pitch of her voice, nothing in her tone belied the urgency of finding out if anyone had been near the crash scene other than the workers present. "Were there police here? Civilians?" If there had been, they would have to be tracked down and quarantined quickly. Susan knew that. She and Christian and Curtis made a good team. They knew their jobs as Macy knew hers.

While her team kept the workers occupied, she had to find the virus.

Slipping away from the group, Macy made her way toward the wreckage. The Learjet looked like a toy that had been smashed by an angry child. Wires snaked out of jagged tears in the plane's skin. Sheets of metal, crumpled like accordions, littered the ground.

She pushed aside the charred skeleton of a seat propped upright in a tangle of shrub, stepped over a man's empty tennis shoe, refusing to wonder what had happened to the foot that had once been inside it. The trickles of sweat slipping down between her breasts became rivers. Her breath sounded huge inside the helmet, roaring through the filter like a hurricane wind, yet outside, there wasn't even enough of a breeze to lift the little red flags marking the locations of human remains.

A lump formed in her throat as she pictured David Brinker beneath one of the white sheets, torn and bloody. David who was so fussy about his appearance.

Who couldn't stand a little dirt under his nails, much less…

Anguish pulled her over to the draped body, but fear wouldn't let her touch it. She bit her lip until she tasted blood. She had to know, she told herself. It was natural to need closure. Besides, she owed it to David, didn't she? To face him one last time.

He wouldn't have been on that plane it hadn't been for her.

Heart racing, she inched closer to the white sheet, the flag at the corner, and glanced around as if she expected David's ghost to materialize. To haunt her for what she'd done.

She told herself she was just being overly emotional. Letting her feelings run away with her again. Still, she couldn't help whispering, "I'm sorry" before reaching for the corner of the covering.

"Sorry for what?" A hand landed on her shoulder.

Macy gasped, straightened and spun with one hand raised to fend off her attacker, even if he was already dead.

The Ranger caught her wrist halfway to his face.

"Whaa—?" She stumbled backward, barely righting herself before she landed on her keester. Blood buzzed in her ears. Her heart raced. She clutched her fist over her chest. "Are you crazy? What are you doing out here?"

"Following you."

"You can't be here. You don't have a suit on." But he had helped himself to a pair of latex gloves from the CDC supplies, she saw.

"I was all over this wreck this morning. If the bug is out here, I've already got it."

"Then you should be in decon." She glanced at the portable showers, now in working order, and the line of workers snaking around them.

"I'll scrub down." His voice was deep and seemed to vibrate deep inside her. It was as almost as unsettling as his eyes. "When it's my turn.

She'd bet a month's pay it wouldn't be his turn until everyone else had finished.

Had he said he'd been following her?

She shook her head as if that would straighten out her jumbled thoughts. "What do you want?"

"The same thing you do."

"Huh?" Brilliant. That implacable stare of his stole her ability to think.

"You're looking for the bug, aren't you?"

No sense in lying. The truth would be written on her face. She'd never been good at deception.

"I want to know what you find." He jerked his head toward the camp. "They're all going to want to know."

He was right. They deserved to know. But what if she found the containment had been breached? How would she tell them?

She pulled in a shuddery breath. "I haven't located the virus yet."

His gray eyes went hard—harder than usual. "Did you think you'd find it under there?" He nodded toward the white sheet.

Heat crawled up Macy's neck to her cheeks. "No. I—" She blew out her breath. "I knew these people. They were my coworkers. My friends." *More.*

"They're dead. Nothing you can do for them now.

Those over there—" He nodded toward the camp. "They're the ones that need your help now."

A wave of guilt hit her—how selfish to be mourning her loss when so many more people—the Ranger included—faced their own mortality. David and his ghost would have to wait.

"The virus was in a steel cylinder about the size of a dormitory refrigerator, shiny and kind of dimpled on the outside, with two combination locks on top. It would have been inside a wooden crate with packing material, but that might have broken away or burned in the crash. Have you seen anything like that around?"

He shook his head, wiping the sheen of sweat off his forehead with the sleeve of his flannel shirt. He didn't seem to mind that the sleeve was as grimy as his face. Again she thought of David and his sterile white shirts. Her stomach plunged.

"Most of the back end of the plane is over there, though." He pointed west. He didn't have to add that a container the size she was looking for would have been stowed in the rear of the aircraft. Didn't have to. The front half was built out with passenger seats, the remains of one of which she was standing on.

She turned and started picking her way in the direction he'd indicated. She heard footsteps behind her, and turned to find him following. "You don't have to come."

"Yes. I do," he said, and she didn't bother to argue. She had a feeling it would be a waste of time.

Since she was wearing what was, for all intents and purposes, a spacesuit, she guessed it was appropriate that she felt as though she was walking on the face of the moon as she picked through the wreckage. She stared at a perfectly pressed pair of trousers hanging in a tree as if left there by a butler. She stepped over a half-completed crossword puzzle as if it were some alien life form. Each bit of debris made her wonder who it had belonged to. What it had meant to them.

Out of the corner of her eye, she watched the Ranger. He walked through the wreckage in a precise criss-cross pattern, his head sweeping left, then right. How did he do it? How did he walk through the remnants of the last moments of five peoples' lives and look so unaffected?

His foot thudded against something metallic. He stopped, rooted in place like a man mired in quicksand. "Doctor?" His head turned, one eyebrow lifted. Then he reached down.

"For God's sake, don't touch it!" She hurried to his side.

"That's it?" he asked when she crouched down next to him.

She nodded, running her gloved hand around the sealed edge. "Looks like it's intact."

"Hallelujah," he said, but without the emotion that should have been attached.

She looked up at him and grinned, feeling like an eight-year-old who'd just caught her first crawfish. "It *is* intact!"

He didn't return her grin. His mouth stayed set in the same firm line. She felt a blush creep up her neck. Of course he wasn't grinning. The unit could still have leaked. The seal would have to be checked microscopically.

He nodded. "Then let's get the hell out of here."

"Fine by me. We'll send a team in to remove it." She marked the sight with orange flagging tape and pushed herself up. He reached out to steady her elbow. The touch sent an electric shock up her arm, even through the cumbersome suit. She took a step back, out of his grasp before she embarrassed herself, and froze.

There, behind the Ranger, a Plexiglas habitat lay cock-eyed in the scrub brush, one of the rubber handling gloves sealed into the hole in its side torn, the other missing altogether. The bolts on one end of the container had been sheared off, and the base ripped away.

The habitat was empty.

"Oh, God," she said, feeling her flush fade as blood drained to her toes.

The Ranger's grip on her arm tightened. "What?"

"The monkey…" She had assumed the animal had been killed in the crash with everyone else aboard.

His gaze swept over the broken habitat. "Animals?"

"One. A rhesus macaque. A research animal."

"Does it pose a danger?"

"It was infected with ARFIS before we left Malaysia." She lifted her gaze to his, then had to turn away from the flat intensity of his stare. From the power swirling in the metallic gray. Dread settled in her chest with the finality of a casket being lowered into a grave. "It's highly contagious."

And now it was loose in Texas. The Sabine National Forest was officially a hot zone.

Chapter 3

Clint's skin was already red from scrubbing off three layers of epidermis in the decontamination shower. As he faced down the smug CDC security guard all dressed up to play soldier in camouflage fatigues, combat boots and a gas mask, even more blood flooded the capillaries just beneath the surface. The fact that Clint was wearing a navy-blue jumpsuit that was two sizes too small and had been told his own clothes were about to be burned, along with everything else he'd had on him this morning, didn't help his disposition any. Neither did the gas mask he held in his left hand, a reminder of the seriousness of the situation here.

"I don't think you understand, son. A Ranger never surrenders his gun and badge. Not while he's still breathing."

"Then you better hope somebody around here knows CPR, 'cause I've already got yours."

"Correction. You've been holding mine while I showered. Now you're going to give them back."

"Correction," Cammo Boy mocked. "Now I'm going to put your badge in the incinerator with the other personal effects. Your weapon—" He turned the plastic bag holding Clint's Glock over in his gloved hands, studying it with a look of admiration. Clint noticed Cammo Boy didn't carry a sidearm, which was a good thing. He didn't look old enough to drive, much less shoot anyone.

Or maybe Clint was just feeling old these days. Old and broken.

"We'll just have to find some other way to dispose of your gun," Guard Boy finished.

Yeah. Like stowing it in his own duffle, Clint imagined. He lifted his hand, fisted it in green camouflage. Before the young guard could so much as blink, the steel toes of the young man's boots were dangling an inch off the ground.

Yancy, the kid's nametag read. He looked like a Yancy. Fancy Yancy. His boots were too clean ever to have seen field duty, and his fatigues actually bore creases. Clint was about to launch young Fancy Yancy into orbit when a voice that sounded as if it came right off an Old South plantation stopped him cold.

"Is there a problem here?" Dr. Attois studied Clint and the security guard, who both spoke at once.

"No."

"Yes."

"Put the corporal down, Ranger Hayes." Behind the plastic face shield, one of the lady doctor's fine eyebrows lifted. "Please."

Grudgingly, Clint set the man on his feet. But he didn't let go of the shirt.

"Uh. Ma'am," Cammo Boy said. "Ranger Hayes is reluctant to proceed to the detainees' waiting area."

"They're not being detained, corporal. They're being quarantined."

"Yes, ma'am. I get that, ma'am. But I'm not sure *quarantinees* is a word, ma'am."

Clint resisted the urge to roll his eyes. "Your rent-a-cop has my weapon, my badge, my boots and my cell phone. I want them back. In that order."

Two bright-red spots colored the man's baby cheeks. "I was ordered to collect all personal effects, ma'am."

"That gun and badge are not personal effects. They belong to the state of Texas. You have no authority—"

"I'm here by order of the federal government. I have more authority than—"

"Gentlemen, please!" The doctor humphed. "We really don't have time for this. Give me his things, Corporal."

"But, ma'am—"

She held out one rubber-gloved hand, planted the other on her neon-orange hip. "Don't make me lose my temper."

If Clint had been much of a smiler—and if he hadn't been so damned aggravated—he might have smiled then. He almost hoped the guard refused to hand over his belongings. It might be kind of fun to find out if the old sayings about hot Cajun blood were true or just another stereotype.

Then again, there were other, more interesting ways to find out how hot the dark-haired, curvy little doctor's blood ran.

Much more interesting ways.

With a discontented sigh and a glare at Clint, the corporal plunked the plastic bags containing his Glock and the silver star and circle that formed the Ranger badge in her outstretched hand.

"Boots?" Clint grunted, mentally chastising himself for letting his mind wander into off-limits territory again—and the doctor's blood, hot or otherwise, was definitely off-limits. He had enough problems at the moment without adding a woman to the mix.

"That's really not a good idea," the woman in question said, the sympathy in her voice as thick as her accent. "Leather holds moisture down in the grain and pores. The virus—"

"I get the picture. Cell phone?"

There was a heavy pause, and then the doctor said, "Walk with me," over her shoulder as she turned, leaving him little choice but to follow, his feet slipping and sliding in the navy-blue rubber galoshes he'd been issued to replace the four-hundred-dollar custom Luccheses that were about to be incinerated. "And put that mask on."

Clint followed, the mask swinging at his side.

"How long have you been in law enforcement, Ranger Hayes?"

She was taking long strides for a woman with short

legs. Like she had a train to catch. The movement had her hips swaying, giving him a picture of the shape inside the bulky orange suit. And quite a shape it was.

He jammed his fingers into the pockets of his jumpsuit. "All total? Sixteen years, I guess."

He wouldn't make seventeen. Either the virus would get him, or he'd have to face his captain, his team, and tell them he wouldn't be coming back from medical leave. At this point, he wasn't sure which outcome he preferred.

"…someone with your experience must understand the need to control the information the public gets about this situation."

He'd missed the first part of what she'd said, but he got her point. "In other words, you're not giving anyone's cell phone back. And it has nothing to do with the virus. Just out of curiosity, what *are* you telling the public?"

"The truth. That a plane carrying hazardous materials crashed in the Sabine National Forest, and that local emergency workers who arrived on scene first are now helping state and federal agencies with the cleanup."

"Helping?" He glanced at the men—mostly farmers and store clerks, mechanics and game wardens. The biggest disaster most of them ever faced was a wreck on the county highway. They weren't prepared for an epidemic. They were sitting around folding metal tables, heads bowed and silent as they listened to a lecture on safety procedures—how to take off latex gloves without cross-contaminating them, leaving their rubber boots outside and stepping into paper booties before they entered their tents, etc. Skip Hollister reached between his feet and plucked a stem of grass, lifted it, then caught himself before he put it in his mouth, tossed it away and ground it under his heel.

"I only need twelve hours before I run the blood tests," the doctor said, following his gaze. Had her eyes teared up? It was hard to tell behind her face shield. "Twenty-four before I can release them back to their families."

"You hope."

She kept walking, marching really, across the compound, but her hands, swinging at her sides, began to clench and unclench rhythmically with each stride. "I have some field-sterilization kits in my tent. They use gas pellets. It'll take a few hours. I'll need you to take your gun apart for me first, and then you'll probably need to clean it to get the residue off before you put it back together, but you'd know better about that than me."

"Not a problem." Not as much of one as being without his gun, anyway. It wouldn't be his much longer, but he didn't want to give it up a second earlier than he had to.

"I'm in the first tent. Come by later and we'll set it up."

She stopped in front of a tent on the far-south end of camp, the opposite direction where she'd said she was quartered. Clint frowned at the two guards posted out front. These two were definitely armed. With automatic weapons and full environmental suits like the doctor's. "How much later?"

The doctor turned to him. Her dark complexion had blanched white except for two red spots on her cheeks that gave her a feverish look. A scary proposition in a camp on the verge of an epidemic.

"Give me an hour or two," she said. Her voice shook, adding to Clint's misgiving. "I have something else to take care of first."

He studied the grim-faced guards behind her. Older, these two. More experienced. They'd seen some things, he was sure. Things they didn't talk about. He could see it in their eyes.

"What else?" he asked.

"It's…not your concern."

"If you're messing with that bug again, out here where there's still innocent people who could be exposed—"

"It's not the virus."

"Then what is this place?"

A wave of torment washed over her expression. "It's the morgue. I have to identify the bodies."

Macy stood frozen inside the flap to the tent housing the temporary morgue. She felt as if her respirator had suddenly quit working. She couldn't draw a breath. Her chest burned, but it wasn't enough to melt the icy shock that encapsulated her, held her immobile as a statue.

There were only three bodies.

She heard a swish of the tent flap behind her, a quiet step, and knew the Ranger had followed her inside. His hand on her shoulder was like an electric shock. It restarted her heart, jolted her lungs. She gulped in a noisy breath.

"What are you doing here?"

"Earlier, you said the people on the plane were your friends." His voice was low, rumbling and hoarse through the gas mask he'd finally donned. "You shouldn't have to do this alone."

Compassion from the Ranger? It didn't seem to fit. But then, maybe there was more to the man than a stony countenance and flat eyes. But she wouldn't bet on it.

"I shouldn't have to do this at all," she said, drawing her mind back to the black bags laid in a neat row. "They shouldn't be here. This shouldn't have happened."

"If man were meant to fly we'd all be born with boarding passes stamped on our foreheads."

Ah, there was the hard-assed Ranger she knew.

"Guard?" she called. When he poked his head inside, she asked, "Where are the others?"

"Other what, ma'am?"

"The other…remains." She couldn't quite think of them as bodies. Bodies belonged to people. What was in those bags belonged to God.

The burly guard frowned. "That's all they found."

Ranger Hayes stepped up beside her. "How many are there supposed to be?"

"Six." Her heart fluttered like a flock of startled sparrows. "You don't think—"

"We searched all around that wreck. There were no survivors," Hayes said, guessing what she was thinking. "Are you sure all six people got on the flight?"

The possibility that it had been a mistake, that David hadn't been on board flared in a ball of bright hope for a moment, then sputtered out.

"I verified it with authorities in Malaysia right after I was notified of the crash." Her eyes grew warm, full. "They're still out there. Somewhere."

"Lot of scavengers out in woods like these. Wouldn't take them long to tear apart a fresh kill, carry off the pieces," the burly guard said.

While images of wolves ripping raw meat off a carcass played in Macy's mind, the Ranger rolled a heavy gaze to the guard. "Thank you, that was very helpful," he said dryly. "That will be all."

The guard ducked out, and Macy walked toward the three black bags. "I need to know who—I need to know."

But her hands stalled on the zipper. The Ranger's hands brushed them away. His eyes were the color of a full moon, his expression just as distant. How did he do it? How did he stand in front of the dead and not so much as blink? A chill ran down her spine as the image of Robocop popped into her head. The half-man, half-machine enforcer had nothing on Clint Hayes.

"I'll open them up," he said. "You just call out the names. I'll take care of the rest."

She wheeled, hating having her weakness on display for a man like the Ranger. This was her responsibility. She wouldn't shirk it. "No!"

He was already pulling at the zipper tab. She pushed him away. "It's my responsibility."

He turned toward her, his brows drawn.

She drew herself up to her full height, diminutive as it was next to his towering frame. "Like I said, they were my friends. I owe it to them."

After a moment's pause, he stepped back, watching her speculatively. Macy reached for the bag again. Her hands shook as she pulled on the zipper tab.

The smell hit her first, even filtered through her respirator, the pungent odor of death that seemed to pull the bile up from her gut like a vacuum pump. She clamped her mouth shut and held her breath, her eyes watering and her chest aching as she edged the bag open another inch. She saw the tattered sleeve of a blue polo shirt caked with coagulated blood and dirt. A dark-skinned hand, abraded and charred, slipped out.

Her breath whooshed out and the zipper whooshed shut at the same time. "It's Cory Holcomb, one of our lab technicians." And the only African-American on-board. At least she hadn't had to look at his face, into his dead eyes, to identify him.

Facing away, gasping for cleaner air she gulped in a few breaths before turning back to the next bag.

"You sure you want to go on with this?" the Ranger asked.

"I have to."

Her heart pounded. Sweat pooled on her palms beneath her rubber gloves. The second zipper eased down though she had no conscious thought of opening it. A shock of blond hair greeted her. A freckled face and a mouth that had once always seemed to be laughing. Now he seemed to be screaming. She could only imagine the terror of his last moments…

Tremors wracking her whole body, Macy reached out and gently pulled his eyelids down over his blue eyes…

"It's Bob Turner, our copilot."

She moved on to the next. "Timlen Zufria, a Malaysian doctor who was working with us."

She zipped the last bag closed and turned, pressing her palm into her stomach to try to calm the churning. The burning. She needed to leave. To run. But the Ranger stood in her way.

"Who else was on board?"

"The pilot, Michael Cain." A tear brushed her cheek. She'd flown with this crew many times. "He has two kids. A girl and a boy."

She wrapped her arms around herself and hugged, mentally shaking herself. The Ranger didn't want to hear her sentimental rambling.

"Ty Jeffries, the man who managed the cargo," she added. "And David Brinker." Her stomach twisted brutally. Unable to stop the rising tide of bile, she pushed Hayes out of her way and ran out of the tent to the edge of the encampment, where she hunkered down behind a scrub mesquite, yanked off her helmet and lost what little food she'd been able to swallow this morning.

Unable to touch her face for fear of contamination, she had no choice but to let the tears flow unabated down her cheeks. As the sobs diminished to hiccups, she heard footsteps crunch through the dry grass behind her. A long shadow fell over her, chilling her clammy skin.

Ranger Hayes squatted down beside her. His gray eyes swirled, unreadable as ever. "Who is David?"

"My fiancé." Misery permeated her every cell. "At least he used to be."

Chapter 4

Clint would rather have stuck his arm in a rattlesnake nest than deal with Dr. Attois now. In his years as a Texas State Trooper, and later as a Ranger, he'd seen a lot of victims, with their wide, shocked pupils and pale faces. He'd learned that doling out sympathy wasn't the way to help them—at least it wasn't his way. He could call in victims' advocates and social workers and counselors for that. The best thing he could do for them was give them justice.

But in an accident, there was no justice to be given, no righteous punishment to be meted, and out here, there were no counselors to call. Whatever had to be done was up to him to do.

She sat on the trunk of a fallen cottonwood, her head bowed. The wet trails scrolling down her cheeks made his breath hitch, his throat close. It made him want to reach out and dry her tears, but he couldn't touch her, not without risking spreading the virus.

Maybe it was for the best. The last thing he needed was to touch her. No, that wasn't true. The last thing he needed was to know whether her skin felt as warm and soft and smooth as it looked or not.

"I'm sorry. I'm sorry." She rocked back and forth, her arms hugging her middle. "It's just—I have a hard time with…the dead."

"Understandable. You said they were your friends."

She shook her head, still rocking herself. "No, I have a hard time with all dead people."

Frowning, Clint squatted down next to her. He spoke as gently as he could manage, but wasn't sure he pulled it off. It had been a long time since he'd tried to be gentle. "Must have made medical school a bitch."

Her laugh came out as a hiccup. "I never would have made it through Advanced Pathology if it hadn't been for the pint of Jack Daniels I kept under my bed. It was the only way I could sleep after…after class."

Full of surprises, the lady doctor was.

She pulled her lips between her teeth then exhaled slowly. "I haven't been able to drink whiskey since I graduated." Her smile trembled then fell. "It tastes like death to me."

Clint felt the meltdown coming a long second before it happened. The sight of tears clumped in her thick lashes twisted through him like a blade. It took all the grit he could muster to keep his own expression impassive.

A moment later, the tide of grief overwhelmed her.

Tears tumbled out, rained to the ground. "I killed David," she cried. "It's my fault."

He shoved his hands, gloves and all, into his pockets to keep them from reaching for her. "You didn't cause the plane to crash."

"I caused him to be on it. He was supposed to come home on the commercial flight, with me, the day before. But I broke off the engagement. I gave him his ring back. He decided to ride back on the charter so he wouldn't have to be around me."

Clint had once served a warrant on a drug house that had turned out to be booby-trapped. The doors were wired with explosives, the windows, the cupboards, even the floorboards were rigged, all in an attempt to kill a few cops. Walking through that house hadn't been nearly as frightening as stumbling through this conversation. He didn't know what to say. He wasn't good at making people feel better.

"By definition, accidents are random events," he said, treading carefully and watching her face for some sign of whether he was helping or making matters worse. "You couldn't have known the plane would go down. Or it could have just as easily been the commercial jet that crashed, and you could have saved his life."

"At least then it would have just been a plane crash. We wouldn't be worrying about an ARFIS epidemic."

"Maybe. Or maybe the plane would have crashed into a school, killed a kid who would have otherwise been president some day. You can't tear yourself up wondering 'what if.' No one knows what the results of their actions will be ahead of time. No one."

If they could—if he could—he sure wouldn't have stepped out of his truck in that parking garage six weeks ago and walked right into two gunmen coming off the elevator. He wouldn't have taken the .38-caliber round in the shoulder that was soon going to change his life forever.

Maybe he wouldn't have stepped up to the front of the crowd when the CDC team had shown up at the crash site, gotten a close-up look at the wild mane of hair, the warm complexion.

Maybe.

Dr. Attois angled her head to the side, a frown tipping her full lips downward as she studied him curiously. Her eyes were the color of chicory coffee, dark and rich. And they were looking at him as if she was seeing a different man than she'd seen the moment before.

Or as if she'd seen more of him than before. The shield he wore over his emotions was slipping. He stood before it came crashing down.

She blinked as if his movement had woken her. The color came back to her cheeks. "I have to find him."

He watched as she stood and pulled on her helmet. "What? Now?"

"I can't leave him out there."

"There's nothing you can do for him."

"I can bring him home! Give him a decent burial, while there's still enough to bury. Before the scavengers…" Her face twisted.

"What about the monkey?"

"Most likely he was killed in the crash. My team is searching the wreckage again for his remains."

"The virus?"

She held out her arms. "I'm protected, remember?"

"That suit'll be shredded about thirty seconds after you leave this clearing. You ever heard of saw briar? Mesquite thorns? Spear grass? These woods are full of them."

She dropped her arms to her sides, took a deep rasping breath through her respirator. "Even if the macaque did survive the crash, which I doubt, it was infected nearly twenty-four hours ago. With its smaller body mass, ARFIS would overwhelm its system much more quickly than it would a human. One way or another, the monkey is dead or soon will be. The virus won't be a threat."

Biting her lower lip, she checked the seals on her wrists and ankles.

He took in her woman-on-a-mission expression and sighed. "At least wait until tomorrow morning. Once the blood tests are done and we're sure no one's sick, we can send the men out in search teams. They may not be big-city doctors, but they know these woods and they're good people. They'll want to help."

"That's a good idea. If I haven't found David and the others by then, we'll do that."

He could tell from her tone that she was only half listening to him. She turned to walk away.

"Damn it," he called to her back, "it's a big forest out there. You can't just go traipsing around it alone."

She laughed, but there was nothing joyous in the sound. "I was raised in the bayou. My sisters and I played so far out in the bogs even the gators couldn't find us. You think I'm afraid of a little walk in the woods?"

As she spoke, she hit the edge of the tree line—and immediately stumbled over a vine that caught her ankle. She caught herself on the trunk of a pine tree just in time to keep from falling on her face, righted herself and disappeared into the foliage.

Cursing his luck and stubborn women under his breath, Clint counted to ten to give his temper a few seconds to cool. Then he counted to ten again.

Finally under control, he yanked the straps on his face mask tight and clomped after her in his rubber booties. The infected monkey might be dead, but the twenty-two men Clint had helped convince to accept the quarantine in the camp behind him weren't. Not yet. If they got sick, they were going to need her.

He'd be damned if he'd let anything happen to her before he knew they were okay.

Either there was a rogue elephant stampeding through the woods behind her, or the Ranger had caught up to her. An awkward moment passed between them when he reached her side. Macy tried to say something, but her throat closed around a knot in her esophagus and she couldn't speak. She flicked him a cautious smile instead.

He must have expected her to be angry at his intrusion, because his eyes rounded in surprise for a moment before the steel curtain he hid behind so often slammed down.

The truth was, she was glad for his company. Under

the canopy of trees, the forest felt like a morgue. The temperature was several degrees cooler. Leaves muffled their footsteps. The critters that should have been scuttling around were quiet, as if in deference to the dead.

She didn't want to be alone with the dead again.

The going was rough, as Ranger Hayes had said it would be. At times the underbrush grew in impenetrable walls. The saw-grass vines seemed alive, reaching out to snag her arms and ankles. Three-inch mesquite thorns sharp enough to puncture the sole of a boot and thick enough to impale a girl to the bone made every step over a broken limb an adventure.

They walked wordlessly until, after nearly an hour, she sat on a mossy boulder near a thin stream to catch her breath.

The Ranger loomed over her, swiveled his head. Sunlight angled through the boughs overhead in sharp beams.

"Gonna be dark before long," he said.

Out of habit she checked the seals between her suit and gloves. "Couple of hours."

"We should head back."

"In a while."

His forehead furrowed over his face mask. "You do know which way is back, don't you?"

"Approximately six-tenths of a mile on a heading of ninety-four degrees."

His scowl deepened. "What're you, a Girl Scout leader wannabe?"

He looked so perplexed that when she smiled this time, it almost felt genuine. She opened her fanny pack, pulled out her Garmin, checked the heading to the way-point she'd made at base, and pointed. "That way."

He leaned over her. "GPS?"

"Part of the standard CDC field pack." She patted the zippered pouch sewn into the waist of her suit. "GPS, satellite phone, two-way text pager. Just because I'm not from the big city doesn't mean I don't appreciate modern technology."

"All right, Techno-Girl. You know where we came from. But do you have any idea where you're going?"

She stood, walked about fifteen feet to her left where there was a break in the trees and pointed up and to the right. "There?"

He followed her outstretched hand with his gaze. Some distance away, six large, black birds glided above the trees. Her stomach plummeted with each heavy swoop of their wings. "Buzzards? You're chasing buz-zards?"

"They're feeding," she said, trying not to picture what lay below them.

"It could be anything. A possum, the remains of a deer some hunter left behind."

"Or one of the men from the plane."

He took her arm in his hand. "Look, we have to get back. We'll call the state. They've got dogs that can search these woods in a fraction of the time it will take us, and do a hell of a better job at it."

"We're almost there."

When she pulled away from him, he made a sound somewhere between a growl and groan and stepped in front of her, this time holding her in place more firmly.

"You don't have to do this yourself. Do you hear me? You do not need to be the one to find your friends."

But his words faded in her mind. Her ears were tuned to another sound. A chirping, trilling chatter. A sound that didn't belong in the quiet woods.

"Shh," she said.

"What?"

"Listen," she whispered, and let her eyes fall partway closed to hone in on the direction of the sound. When she opened them again, she pointed over the Ranger's shoulder. "There."

He turned, and the color blanched from his skin. His hand gripped her arm with bruising force.

In a tree twenty feet away, a black-and-white ball of fur scampered out a limb and plucked a nut from a twig, gnawed on it, chattered some more and threw its prize to the ground.

"I'm no doc, doc," the Ranger said in the most un-emotional tone she'd heard from him yet. "But that monkey doesn't look dead to me."

No. Not dead.

Not even close.

Chapter 5

Clint's right hand reached for the weapon he always carried on his hip and came up empty.

"Impossible." Dr. Attois's words were barely audible. She crouched and held out one hand toward the cat-size ball of fur with the pink nose on the tree limb. The monkey mimicked her gesture, holding out its paw. "Here, little monkey, monkey. Here, José."

"What are you doing?" Clint tried to watch the animal, but all he could see was the puncture on the thigh of the doctor's biohazard suit. The tear near her elbow. She'd have been better off with a simple gas-mask-type of device such as Clint wore—wasn't wearing, actually, he realized, and yanked the device over his face, tightening the straps until they cut into the back of his head.

Wouldn't matter if her clothes were torn to shreds if

she had a mask like his that sealed airtight around her face so the virus couldn't get in her lungs, or the mucous membranes of her eyes or nose.

"Come here, José. Come on, little guy."

"José?"

"The monkey."

An Hispanic monkey from Malaysia. Carrying the most lethal virus of this decade.

Jesus.

Clint checked the straps around his face, tightened them another fraction of an inch. A rivulet of sweat ran down his temple and lodged against the rubber seal at his jaw. "What are you going to do with it if you catch it? You've got holes all over your suit."

"It's all right. We're upwind of him. The virus will be drifting the other way. I just need to get close enough for him to see the food." She dug gently in the zippered pouch at her waist. Paper crinkled, and out came a granola bar. She eased the wrapper off and set the bar on the ground in front of her. "If he finds food here, he's more likely to stay in the area."

"Fine. Great." The trickle of sweat from his forehead was becoming a river. He was going to drown in his face mask if they didn't get out of here soon. "Let's go."

The monkey scampered down the tree trunk and took a tentative step toward Dr. Attois, then another. She rose and backed away slowly, stopping to dig in her pouch again, this time pulling out her GPS.

"What are you doing?" Clint hissed.

"Marking a waypoint so we can give the exact coordinates to a recovery team."

"You're calling in a recovery team?"

"I have to. We need to know why he's not dead, or at least seriously ill."

"Terrific." Of course he'd known that. Someone would have to come back for the monkey. Many some-ones, most likely, in order to find one tiny monkey in a wilderness this size. And every one of them would be risking their lives with each breath they took, regard-less of how much protective gear they wore.

"Any more bad news?"

"Yeah." She studied the leaves twirling on brittle branches. "The wind is changing direction."

Just out of his second decontamination shower of the day, Clint strode across the compound toward Dr. At-tois's tent in a stride meant to chew up gravel and spit out dust. Once they'd called in the coordinates on Macy's satellite phone, they'd run like hell all the way back to camp. With Macy's ripped suit, they'd have been crazy to stick around and wait for the recovery team—a fancy name, Clint had learned for a group of sharpshooters with tranquilizer guns.

Already, news that the infected monkey was alive and well in the woods of southeast Texas had the clear-ing housing the quarantined workers and their CDC captors buzzing with activity. The news that the recov-ery team sent after José hadn't found hide nor hair of the animal at the coordinates Macy had given them had everyone's nerves jumping.

Three more helicopters had arrived, dropping off ad-ditional equipment and troops. The evening sun had set, and generators droned like overgrown yellow jackets, powering the monstrous lights that had been set up to keep the night at bay. Motion sensors were in place to detect even the smallest breach—inbound or outbound—of the camp's perimeter, and in case those failed, the uniformed guards with rifles surrounding the little circle of tents were sure to do the trick.

Two more of the army that had invaded the once-quiet forest stood sentry outside Dr. Attois's tent. There was no mistaking these guys for CDC office drones or scientists, or even young hotheads like Cammo Boy. They were professional security. Thick-necked grunts with guns on their hips and chips on their shoulders.

Clint marched right up to them, stopping a little too close, invading their personal space to see if they'd take a step back.

They didn't. He hadn't really thought it would be that easy to establish himself as alpha dog, but it was worth a try.

"I need to see Dr. Attois," he announced, hating the nasal sound the breathing filter added to his voice.

"She's not available."

"She'll see me."

A guard with three stripes on his shoulder, apparently the senior officer of the two, gave him a condescending smile. "We'll tell her you'd like to speak with her. When she's available. *Ranger* Hayes."

So, they'd already been briefed on him, and this was how they wanted to play it. Get into a pissing contest over who had the bigger badge.

That was all right. He could piss pretty damned far.

He leaned around the big guy's shoulder and called, "Dr. Attois, you in there?"

"You'll have to leave now," the junior guard ordered. "Civilians are not to leave their tents for the duration."

"I'm not a civilian."

"You can either return to your tent on your own, or we'll escort you there."

The senior guard's tone left no doubt in Clint's mind that "escort" meant "drag." The young guy latched a rubber-gloved hand on Clint's shoulder.

Clint knocked his arm away with a chop to the inside of the elbow. "Back off."

"Go back to your assigned tent."

Both guards advanced on Clint. Holding his ground, he looked the bigger of the two, the leader, in the eye and balanced on the balls of his feet, fists clenched. "Dr. Attois! I need to speak to you. Now!" he yelled without taking his eyes off the guards.

The junior man grabbed Clint's arm, tried to leverage it behind his back. Clint twisted in an escape maneuver, but before he got away, the senior guard leaned on his back, doubling him over, and smashed a knee into Clint's face. Warm blood gushed from his nose. "Aw, now look what you've done," he whined, still bent over, trying to plug his nose and hoping to baffle them just long enough to get the jump on them. "Gone and ruined my pretty blue jumpsuit."

The distraction worked. The guards rocked back on their heels, thinking the fight was over. Rage thundering in his chest, Clint bulled forward with his head down, knocking the junior guard to the ground. He shoved the other one behind him and aimed a backward kick at his groin, missing by inches when the man slid aside.

"Stop it. Stop it now!"

The voice was feminine, but there was no doubting the authority in its tone. The guard behind Clint took a step back. The guard on the ground staggered to his feet.

Clint straightened and turned his attention to Dr. Attois, wiping his bloody nose with his sleeve. "I need a word with you."

"You're hurt." She threw a challenging look at the guards.

"I'll live," Clint mumbled into his sleeve.

"He refused to return to his quarters, ma'am."

Clint tipped his head back to stem the flow of blood. "All due respect, doctor, this is a quarantine camp, not a penitentiary."

She'd taken off her rubber suit and wore Keds, faded jeans and a soft, fuzzy lavender sweater that made his body hum in purely male appreciation. He wondered how blood could still be running from his nose when it felt as though all of it had shot to his groin.

Watching him with curious eyes, she stepped back from the tent flap. "Come inside."

"Ma'am—" the senior guard complained.

"Enough, Carter," she said simply as Clint took a step forward.

She stopped him with a hand on his chest. "Take off the booties and gloves and put them in the biohazard container outside. Then step into the pan of disinfectant so you don't track anything in on the bottom of your feet and clean your hands, all the way up past the elbow, with the solution on the table."

He'd just left decon, but he followed orders without comment. Inside, a cool breeze chilled the sweat on Clint's forehead. He rolled his eyes down until he could see something besides the ceiling and sighed appreciatively. The tents were more like big balloons than traditional camping equipment. They were mushroom shaped, sealed up tight, and each had its own air-filtration system. They reminded Clint of an old movie about a boy with no immune system who couldn't ever leave his hermetic environment for fear of infection.

Dr. Attois pulled a chair out from a folding table and motioned him toward it. He stood, surveying the neat cot and blanket, table and laptop computer. "Nice place. If you don't mind living like the boy in the plastic bubble."

"Beats dying." She dug through a footlocker and came up with a hand towel and a bottle of hydrogen peroxide. "Now are you going to sit down or do I have to do this standing on my tiptoes?"

She held the bottle of peroxide up. He reached for it. "I can do it myself."

She pulled the disinfectant out of his reach and nodded to the chair again. "I'm sure you can. But I'm the doctor, remember. Now sit."

Reluctantly, he sat. Arguing with her wasn't going to get him anywhere.

She clucked over him as she cleaned around his mouth. "Now what's so important that you'd risk bodily harm just to talk to me?"

For a moment he couldn't remember. She leaned over him, and all he could see was the milky column of her throat. She smelled like Ivory soap and her fingers were soft and gentle as they worked. It had been a long time since anyone had touched him so personally. Since a woman had touched him at all.

He couldn't help but notice every detail about her as she worked over him. The way the light caught her eyes when she smiled. The way she touched the tip of her tongue to her upper lip when she was concentrating. His heartbeat thrummed heavily in his veins, as if his blood had turned to mercury.

The unexpected reaction to her chafed him. This after only a few hours in her company? By the time the quarantine was lifted—if it was lifted—he'd be lucky if he was capable of speech.

He cleared his throat. *Telephone.*

"I need to use your satellite phone."

She pulled back from him. The scent of Ivory wafted away, just out of reach. He caught himself just before he leaned forward to capture it again. "I'm afraid that's not possible. Tilt your head back."

When he didn't comply, she eased his forehead backward with the heel of her hand and dabbed at his nostrils with a gauze pad. He grabbed her wrist. Was it his imagination, or did her pulse leap under his fingers?

Their gazes met. Her pupils widened. No, it hadn't been imagination.

He let her go, easing her back slightly in the same motion. "Look, I need to call my office. Let them know where I am."

She yanked her gaze away and turned her back to him to put her supplies away. A warning buzz replaced the drumbeat in Clint's veins.

"I'm sorry," she said. "I can't let you use the phone. There's a media blackout. It's against—"

"I'm not going to call the media. I'm going to call the Rangers. The search for your damn monkey is going to be huge. There are dozens of little towns surrounding the national forest. The evacuation alone is going to eat up nearly every law-enforcement resource in the state. I have to make sure there're enough cops ready to back us—"

She wheeled. They stood so close that the top of her head was practically under his chin. Her mouth was just inches below his. It opened to speak, paused. He felt the warm rush of her breath. Smelled her mint toothpaste.

"There isn't going to be an evacuation," she said. Worry lines fanned out from the corners of her chicory-coffee eyes and her mouth.

"What do mean, *no evacuation?*"

With one last, suffering look, she ducked away. Her hands shook as she screwed the cap on the peroxide bottle and shoved the bloody gauze into a plastic bag.

"They—" She cut herself off, stumbling over her words. "It's safer if everyone just stays in their homes," she claimed, sounding as though she was reading a prepared statement. Or propaganda. She kept her eyes carefully averted and her hands busy, closing the first aid kit and stowing it in her trunk.

He forced his clenched fists to relax. His right hand trembled, and he jammed the fingers into his pocket.

Hiding the tremor in his voice wasn't so easy. It took every one of his years of self-discipline to accomplish the task.

"There's no reason to cause a panic," she said. "When we find the animal—"

"*If* you find the animal."

"We'll find it."

"Before or after it wanders into a schoolyard and kills the whole first-grade class, or leaves a trail of virus down Main Street as it picks through the garbage cans looking for something to eat?"

She bit down on her lower lip. He paced the tent, tilting his head back when he felt a slow trickle of blood again in his nostril. "You don't agree with this, do you?"

"It doesn't matter what I think. The decision has been made."

"By whom?"

"The head of the CDC, the Secretary of Health and Human Services, the President." She shrugged her shoulders. "Who knows? All I know is the call came down from someone with a lot more clout than me."

"Your chimp is mobile. There's no guarantee he's going to stay in the forest. He could be anywhere by now."

"Which is exactly why an evacuation isn't a good idea. If one of them is already infected, and carries the virus out of the area…" She didn't have to describe the epidemic that could sweep across the U.S. as easily as it had devastated Malaysia. "People are being warned that there is a dangerous animal in the area. They're being asked to call in if they see him. That's all we can do for now."

"*Dangerous* animal?" He got a sick feeling in the pit of his stomach. "What are you telling them?"

She pulled her lips between her teeth and looked away again. Oh no, she didn't agree with this policy. "They're being told the macaque is rabid."

"Rabid? Who made that decision, some yahoo in Washington?" He stopped his pacing right beside her and loomed over her. "Lady, this is huntin' country. You tell people there's a rabid monkey running loose, every lovin' one of them is going to grab their .22s and pile in their pickup trucks and go look for it. You want to keep them in their houses, you've got to warn them about the virus."

"They're afraid of starting a panic."

"You think they're not going to panic when they see a few hundred cops and military and whoever else descend on this area to search for your rabid monkey? You think they're not going to get suspicious?"

"We're being as discreet as possible."

Disbelief made Clint's shoulders droop. "Don't tell me. There's not going to be a search, either."

She jerked her head to the side in one sharp motion. "Not a massive one like you describe. We've got a couple dozen CDC people and a special biohazard squad from Fort Hood coming in to set traps in the forest. If we're lucky, we won't have to find the macaque. He'll find us."

"That's a mighty big 'if.'" He couldn't hold back the scowl that crawled across his forehead. "Christ, I've got to get out of here." He had to warn people. He headed for the exit, but she stopped him.

"You'll never make it. Security—"

He spun on his heel and loomed over her. "Screw security. Your agency is playing games with thousands of lives because you don't want to admit that you lost a research monkey that could start an epidemic. It's politics, not precaution, and you know it. You're more worried about losing your federal funding than keeping the people here alive."

She flinched as if he'd slapped her. "I—I told you. It's not my decision. I'm a scientist. I don't make policy."

He wanted to grab her. Shake her. Instead he took a deliberate step back. Two deep breaths. Cool-hand Clint, always in control. "But you don't agree with the policy, do you?"

A heartbeat passed. He saw panic scroll through her eyes, then resignation.

He wouldn't make her say it out loud. Didn't need to hear it when he saw the truth swirl in her coffee eyes.

"Then help me do something about it. Who are you working with on a state level?" Texans were more likely to care about Texans than any federal agencies. "The Department of Public Health? The Federal Emergency Management Agency? Who?"

"My director said he'd been in contact with the governor."

The first ribbon of relief curled through Clint. "If the governor's in on it, then you can bet he's called in the Rangers."

He waited for that to sink in.

"Will they be told the truth, at least?"

"As far as I know."

"Then I need to call my office," he said, forcing a soft urgency to his voice. "Let them know they've got a man inside."

"I was given a direct order…"

"Damn it, do you want to stop this disaster from happening, or not?"

Her eyes glistened.

He held out his hand. "Then give me your phone."

No response. But he could see her thinking about it.

"Or you could suddenly feel the need to get some fresh air. I could stay here, with my head tipped back until the bleeding stops. You wouldn't be responsible if I were to find your communications gear and use it without your permission."

Temper flared in her dark irises. "You think that little of me? That I have to hide behind deniability?"

He waited, his heart crashing in his chest, trying not to admire her forthrightness. Or the way her chest heaved beneath her sweater. "Does that mean you're going to help me or not?"

She went to the table and dug through a canvas backpack, finally pulling out what looked like a clunky cell phone. She held it out, but didn't quite put it in his hand. "If I'm going to disobey an order, I do it straight up. No excuses. No deniability. You have five minutes. Make your call."

With that, she gave him the phone, slid on a face mask and a pair of latex gloves, slipped a set of booties over her shoes and walked out of the tent. As he watched her go, Clint couldn't help but think that the spirit inside that curvy little body was as enchanting as the rest of her.

And that he was in deep, deep trouble on a lot of levels.

Chapter 6

"Hayes, where the hell are you?" Texas Ranger Company G Captain "Bull" Matheson answered his cell phone on the fourth ring.

Even with a hundred miles between them, Bull's tone made Clint wince. He was glad they weren't face to face. When he was pissed off, Captain Matheson's ice-blue stare had a way of making a man feel about as small as a midget's boot heel, and he definitely sounded pissed off at the moment.

"I've been trying to call you all day. You were supposed to have been back at work yesterday."

"It's…kind of a long story, Cap."

There was commotion in the background. Shouts. Hurried footsteps. Slamming doors and ringing phones. If Bull was in the office, it sounded like the place was in chaos. "Well, wherever you are, get your ass back here now and bring your outdoor gear. Muster at Love Field in three hours. We're backing up E Company in East Texas. We got a bad situation down there."

"That's an understatement," Clint said quietly.

Bull paused to give an order to someone on his end of the line. "How the hell do you know? I just found out myself ten minutes ago."

"I'm here already."

Another pause, this one longer. Silent. "Where, exactly," the captain said, enunciating carefully, "are you?"

"Ground zero. I saw the plane go down. Came out to see what I could do. Now I'm stuck in quarantine."

"Damn it, Hayes…"

"I know, Cap." Clint squeezed his eyes shut for a second. "I know."

An awkward silence followed, broken only by mutual deep breaths. Clint figured the captain had no more idea what to say than he did. They both knew the possibilities. The Malaysian death toll from ARFIS had been big news for months.

"What's the situation there?" Bull finally asked, his voice rougher than usual.

Clint opened his eyes, focused on the job at hand. "The camp is secure, for now. CDC brought in their own people, but I'm not sure these guys are going to be able to handle it if things get ugly."

"All right." Clint heard the captain's measured footfalls, knew he was pacing. He always did when he was thinking. And when he was worried. "You're my eyes and ears in there. I want to know what's happening. You have to keep things under control and you're going to have to do it on your own. I'm not going to be able to send you any help."

"I know. What's going on outside?"

"The park has been cleared of hikers and campers, roads in and out are closed. National Guard is on alert and the governor has called out all seven Ranger companies—every damn Ranger in the state—to move into the area just in case." He didn't have to say *just in case what*.

"Cap, you've got to convince the governor to order an evacuation."

Bull swore. "Tried already. Don't know what the hell the politicos are thinking, but the stand-down orders are coming from way up the chain. Somewhere in Washington, I think."

"Washington doesn't run the state of Texas. The governor can override them."

"And end his political career doing it. He's not going to take that chance without damn good reason."

"The lives of his constituents aren't reason enough?"

"That's not what I meant, Hayes, and you know it. This thing is a jurisdictional nightmare. The CDC, FEMA, the Department of Public Health, the National Transportation Safety Board—they're all arguing over who's in charge. Even Homeland Security and the Department of Defense are involved. The governor can't just go reversing their orders. If he were to be wrong, and an evacuee carried the virus to another county or state, this thing could be out of control in no time."

Clint shook his head, pinching the bridge of his nose. "It's already out of control, Bull. Way out of control."

"Do what you can, Clint. You've got to keep a lid on things there."

"I know."

"I'll want regular status reports from you."

"I know that, too."

The captain grunted an acknowledgement. Or maybe it was an order to someone on his end. Clint figured he'd accomplished his mission and started saying his good-byes. He was ready to hang up, but the captain didn't seem ready to break the connection.

"When this is over," Bull said after a long, awkward pause, "I'm going to want to hear that long story about what you're doing in East Texas responding to plane crashes when you were supposed to be at work in Dallas."

"I hope I live to tell it, Bull." Clint's jaw hardened. "I hope I live to tell it."

The captain blew out a breath. "Hayes, there's a doctor there with you."

"Attois." The name rolled off his tongue a little too easily to suit him.

"According to the briefing I got from the governor, she knows everything there is to know about this bug."

A wan smile curled across Clint's lips. "Except how to kill it. Guess she forgot that little detail when she decided to bring it to the United States."

"Don't blame this mess on her. She didn't fly that plane into the ground. I want you to stick with her, Clint. If this thing heats up, she's the one they're going to turn to to stop it. I want to know what she knows. You get intel from her, you pass it on to me." He grunted. "I'll make sure the governor gets it, and we'll see about that evacuation."

Clint started to object to the order to stick to Macy Attois. But even as he opened his mouth, his body began to hum. Before he could stop it, the images of her dark eyes, fringed with heavy lashes, the curve of her jeans—and how she would look without them—stole into his mind.

He sighed. "Is that an order, Cap?"

"You got some problem with the doctor?"

"Problem? No, no problem," Clint said dryly, thinking about the view he'd had of her backside as she'd stepped out of the tent. He hadn't meant to notice the gentle roll of her hips when she walked.

Hadn't meant to, but had. In a big way. Even with everything else on his mind. It didn't make sense.

"Damn it, Clint. Don't screw around with her."

He slammed the door in his mind to the images of doing just that. "Don't worry, Captain."

He disconnected the call. Him and Dr. Attois?

Wasn't going to happen. No way, no how.

He kept telling himself that, even as she walked back into the tent, fine eyebrows lifted in silent question, and he found himself incapable of tearing his gaze away from the soft spread of her chest against the folded air mattress and blankets she held in her arms.

"I pitched the ball," he answered her unspoken question. "We'll see if anybody catches it. Why the hell is that monkey still alive, anyway?"

"I don't know. I can't explain it. Maybe the cells he was injected with were mishandled, and he was never infected at all. Maybe the virus has mutated somehow." Her brows furrowed, then lifted. "I do have some good news, though. The blood tests on the work crew were all negative."

He blew out a breath. "Maybe there is a God."

And maybe not, since Dr. Attois bent over to set her bedding down right in front of him. He made a retreat toward the door before he found himself staring at her backside the way he'd ogled her front.

"Let's hope so." She glanced over her shoulder at him. "And let's hope his favor holds out twelve more hours until you and I are in the clear."

Even the sight of her rounded little rear end shining up at him couldn't stop that statement from garnering his full attention. "What?"

Her hands stilled where she was busy spreading the mattress and blankets into a pallet. "We could have been exposed today. I mean, I'm sure we'll be fine, but…. It'll be morning before we'll know for sure. In the meantime, it looks like you and I will be spending the night to-gether."

The Ranger didn't say a word, but his stiff expression made Macy feel that he'd rather jump into a pool of leeches than spend the night with her.

Well, why shouldn't he? Jennifer Lopez she was not. And there was the little matter of her being responsible for an epidemic that could kill thousands of his friends and neighbors.

Not to mention the Ranger himself.

Suddenly embarrassed, she turned away from him, moved across the tent and busied her hands at the instant coffeemaker that had seen more of the world than most diehard travelers. She filled the battered carafe from a gallon jug of water on the floor. "I'm sorry I can't provide better accommodations, but the Ritz was all booked. There's an air pump in the footlocker."

She glanced over her shoulder without thinking about it, found him staring at her and shuddered.

How could a man's expression be so inscrutable and his eyes so…penetrating? She'd never been good at hiding what she was feeling, but when the Ranger looked at her, she was sure he could read her every thought.

Given what she'd been thinking when she'd made up a bed for him, she found the possibility distinctly uncomfortable.

He eyed the pallet, dragged a hand through his close-cropped hair and blew out a breath. "Guess it could be worse. I was assigned to a tent with Skip Hollister."

A harsh laugh burst out of her. "Glad to know I'm not *quite* the bottom of the roommate barrel."

"He snores like a freight train."

"How do you know I don't?"

He eyed her up and down, bringing the blood up her neck. "Do you?"

"You won't have to worry about it tonight." She pulled her lower lip between her teeth, the seriousness of their situation eating its way through her mind like slow poison. "I doubt I'll be sleeping much."

He didn't ask why. Guess he didn't have to.

Without a clue what to do next, she sat on the edge of her cot while he blew up his air mattress, then realized she still had the coffee carafe in her hand and got up to pour the water in the reservoir. Her nerves didn't need the caffeine, but she didn't know what else to do with herself. The Ranger finished inflating his bed about the same time the coffeemaker quit gurgling.

After he put the pump away, she handed him a cup and reached for another mug for herself. "I don't have any sugar or cream."

"Black is fine. Thanks."

They both stared into their coffee in silence. The Ranger sipped, blew the steam off the cup and drank again.

She wrapped her fingers around the mug, absorbing its warmth. Time seemed to thicken. To pass the way molasses poured from a bottle. Painfully slowly. At this rate, morning would never come.

Macy sat on the edge of her cot again, fiddled with her cup. "So, what were you doing responding to a plane crash out in the middle of nowhere in the middle of the night? Seems like a strange place to find a Texas Ranger."

He paced to the door of the tent, back. "We go where we're needed."

"Big crime wave in Hempaxe, Texas, population 384, is there?"

"I was…on leave. Staying at a cabin on Lake Farrell. Saw the plane go down."

"Skip Hollister said he knew you when you were a boy. Did you grow up around here?"

He shook his head. "Just summers."

"Where did you live the rest of the year?"

"You got a sudden desire to write my memoir?"

"Just trying to make conversation."

He stared at her a moment, then shook his head. "Sorry. Cop habit, not giving out personal information. The cabin belonged to my grandpop. I visited for a couple of months in the summer, traveled all over the world repairing oil rigs with my dad the rest of the year."

"You didn't have a permanent home?"

"Just hotels and oil-field bunkhouses."

Pity twisted through her chest like a corkscrew. She couldn't imagine moving all the time. Not having a place to call home. A doorframe to notch the kids' heights in as they grew.

She wanted to tell him she was sorry, comfort him somehow, but he neatly changed the subject before she had a chance.

"What about you?" he asked. "What did you do as a kid, besides play so far out in the bayou the gators couldn't find you."

She smiled as she remembered throwing that tidbit of her childhood over her shoulder at him as she'd marched off into the woods that afternoon. It was true, if a bit of an exaggeration.

"How does a girl from the bayou wind up as a virus hunter for the CDC?"

"What better place to learn about bugs than the bayou? The ones I play with now are just a lot smaller." The warmth of the coffee spread through her chest along with memories of happier days. "Truth is, there was a time when I wanted nothing more than to hang out my shingle as a family doctor in some small town where I could make a difference."

"So why didn't you?"

"Sometimes fate has other plans for us."

And sometimes we're too afraid to poke our heads out of our shells and see what fate has in store.

After a disastrous affair with a visiting surgeon who'd told her he loved her, but neglected to mention the wife and two kids waiting for him in California during her second-year residency, Macy had found the solitary world of viral research science comforting. Unlike people, viruses were predictable. They could be studied. Understood. The laboratory environment, with its bulky suits and airtight work chamber provided her some necessary emotional distance from her coworkers.

Even her relationship with David had been cool. Sterile. He had appreciated her for her mind. She liked his ambition. If there wasn't much chemistry between them, there was at least safety.

She'd thought safety was enough, until recently when she'd found herself awake until all hours, reading steamy romance novels and crying over old Bogart and Bacall movies.

Like a tulip bulb that had lain dormant in the frozen ground until spring, she found herself slowly coming to life. Reaching for the sun. Warmth.

She needed heat in her life. Passion. Laughter and tears. So she'd broken off her engagement to David. And now he was dead, and here she was with the Ranger, the wrong kind of man for her in the wrong place at the wrong time…and all she could think was she wished he would put his arms around her. Just hold her for a moment.

Like that was going to happen.

Embarrassed to realize her eyes had filled with tears—and that the Ranger had reached down to wipe them away with his thumb—she swiped at her face with the sleeve of her sweater and sniffed. He pulled his hand back, his inscrutable expression unchanged, but the air between them had changed. Charged.

"I suppose you've always known you wanted to be a Texas Ranger. Life never threw you any curves?"

"Until recently."

How could she have forgotten? She'd sat here wallowing in her own misery as if his life—or death—didn't hang on a simple blood test to be performed in the morning. Without thinking she reached out and took his hand. His fingers were warm. There was heat inside him, after all. She wondered if there was passion, as well, beneath the stoic exterior, then chastised herself for the direction of her thoughts.

Wrong man. Wrong place. Wrong time.

He eased his hand from hers, but when he walked away, his back seemed more rigid, his gait stiffer. She wished she could reassure him everything would be all right, but she couldn't be sure it would. Besides, he obviously didn't want her comfort.

Deciding not to poke the wounded bear, she sighed,

dug through her footlocker for the playing cards she always carried on field missions, and laid out the first of many hands of solitaire.

Clint twitched at the sound of every voice outside the tent. Jumped at every footstep that sounded as if it might be coming his way.

The sun had come up an hour ago. Dr. Attois's assistant, Susan, a large-boned woman with a wide mouth, had taken blood samples from both him and the doctor shortly thereafter. The tests should be done any minute.

"Pacing isn't going to bring Susan back any quicker."

She was still sitting on her cot playing solitaire. Said it relaxed her.

He hadn't said so, but he found her choice of distraction sad. She shouldn't need to play card games alone to relax. Wouldn't need to, if she was his woman.

But she was not his woman. Never would be. Not in this lifetime.

However long or short that might prove to be.

Dragging his hand through the roots of his hair, he started back across the tent that seemed to be shrinking by the minute, then whirled when he heard the zipper on the outside tent flap open. A tall, blond guy in a full environmental suit stood outside the clear interior tent flap, which was still secured.

That couldn't be good, could it?

Dr. Attois unfolded herself from her cot and hurried over. "Curtis?"

"Just wanted to let you know that Christian and I

have finished screening all the workers. None of them are showing any symptoms, and their blood is still clean. They're good to go."

"Excellent."

"Still no sign of José, but the military dropped a hundred traps baited with fruit into the woods last night within a three-mile radius of where you saw him. He's got to get hungry. We'll get him."

"Good," Dr. Attois said. Was Clint imagining it, or did her voice sound strained?

"Yeah," the man she'd called Curtis said, and turned to leave. "It is."

Two steps away, he stopped and looked back at them. "Oh, I almost forgot. Susan asked me to tell you she finished your blood work." He peered at them solemnly through his face shield, then cracked a wide grin. "No virus. You're in the clear."

Dr. Attois's breath shot out of her chest. She charged the door, grabbing for her gas mask. "Curtis Leahy, I'm going to kill you when I get out there!"

But she was smiling as she threatened him. He just laughed and strode away with a wave.

She dropped her mask back onto the table and turned, nearly running into Clint. He put his arms out instinctively to balance her. She wrapped hers around his back and squeezed.

"We're clear. Did you hear? We're clear! I knew everything would be all right."

At the moment, Clint was anything but all right. The news that he and the doctor both had dodged the ARFIS bullet had his heart in high gear. That, and the press of her plump breasts against his chest, the friction of her thighs scraping against his as she hopped up and down on her toes in joy, had his blood roaring, his hands wandering from her shoulders to her back, then lower, and his mind conjuring up crazy possibilities about the two of them. Right here. Right now.

What better way to celebrate life?

She tipped her head back to look at him through the corkscrew locks of dark hair that shuttered her seductress' eyes, to smile at him, and—

Oh, hell. Stifling a groan, he lowered his lips to hers. Kissed her. Tasted her. Memorized the shape and texture of her.

And realized that he'd dodged one bullet this morning, only to have another, in the form of a sexy, sassy little doctor, strike him dead in the heart.

Chapter 7

Macy's body softened like warm wax under the Ranger's onslaught of a kiss. Her senses were overwhelmed with his woodsy smell, the feel of hard muscles and heat. Had she wondered if there was heat in him? There was fire inside this man. Molten lava, bubbling, unseen but felt, just below the surface of that stoic exterior.

How did he hide it so well?

Why did he hide it at all?

What was she doing thinking when there was so much to *feel,* to experience? To enjoy.

She stretched up onto her toes to give him fuller access. His hands slid down her back, pulling her closer, leaving her skin tingling along their trail. His hips surged forward, tantalizing her with an intimate impression of him against her thigh.

Oh, my.

"Macy, we need to know what you want to tell— Oh. Ahem."

Macy jumped away from the Ranger, dizzy. Her thoughts whirled. Her senses shorted out for a moment at the sudden loss of the high-voltage charge they'd been receiving only a moment before.

Susan stood outside the clear plastic tent seal, her cheeks as red as strawberries behind her face mask. "Sorry to interrupt."

Gathering herself, Macy tugged her sweater down and cleared her throat. "You weren't interrupting. We were just— That is—" She looked over her shoulder for help, found none. "We got a little carried away with the good news. What is it you said you needed?"

Susan's gaze jumped from Macy to the Ranger and back. "Umm—"

"It's okay. Whatever it is, he can hear it."

"We need to know what you want to tell the workers. Some of them are asking about going home."

Macy studiously avoided looking back at the Ranger. "Ask them to be patient a little while longer."

Susan nodded as she backed away. "Yeah. Sure. Okay."

Macy could feel the Ranger behind her. The air vibrated with his presence. Or maybe that was her, shaking in her tennis shoes.

"You're not going to let them go, are you?"

A moment ago, she would have given this man her body, if he'd asked. The least she could do now was give him the truth. "I can't."

"You can't keep them here forever."

"Just until we catch the monkey."

"*If* you catch the monkey."

"We'll get him. But we can't let the men go back to town until we do."

"Because they know the truth," Clint said.

"They'll start a panic."

"Maybe you should have thought about that when you decided to lie to the public, to tell them you were out here looking for a *rabid* monkey, to begin with."

"I didn't lie to anyone. I put my career on the line, trying to help you get the truth out, if you remember. And besides, I'm not just keeping them here because I don't want them talking in town."

His eyelids flickered, almost imperceptibly. It wasn't much, but she interpreted it as intrigue. He wondered what she was up to, she realized, and took some small measure of satisfaction in the fact that she recognized it.

Maybe the Ranger's control wasn't so iron-clad after all. He showed his emotions, if subtly. A girl just had to pay attention, and know how to read them.

She was learning.

"You said they were good men," she answered his unspoken question. "They know these woods. They know how to hunt, to track animals. I've got a bunch of city boys out there, and we've got a hundred traps to check, and keep checking until we catch that monkey. If we pair them up, they'll make better time, cover more ground." She looked at him through her lashes. "I need their help. Assuming your guys are willing."

"You give them protective gear, they'll be willing. This is their town that monkey has put at risk."

"We'll give them gear, but I won't lie. There are still risks. Comes with the job."

"Some things are worth the risk. I figure their town, their families fall into that category." He trailed along on her heels, watching her gather her gear. "You're going out there, too, aren't you?"

"I wouldn't ask my people—or yours—to do anything I wouldn't do myself." She pressed her lips thin. "Besides, it might be their town, friends, neighbors and families, but it's my damned monkey. My virus."

He picked up his respirator and followed her to the door. "Then I guess you're going to need a partner, too, partner."

She turned and looked up at him, her heart going soft and slushy. "Fate's smiled on you twice. You sure you want to test her again?"

"I'm a Texas Ranger. I live to test fate."

"Is that why you kissed me, *Ranger* Hayes?" The words popped out before she could stop them. Mortified, she stared at the ground.

He lifted her chin with a finger. She hadn't realized how close they were. How large he was. How daunting.

His pupils dilated a fraction. His lips parted and she thought he might kiss her again, but instead he said, "No. But since we do seem to have moved beyond the handshake and formal greeting stage, *Macy,* maybe you could call me Clint."

He dropped her chin. She wanted to ask why he had

kissed her, if it hadn't been to test fate, but she couldn't seem to form the words. Could barely think coherently.

But she did remember one thing. Under the table behind her sat a plain stainless-steel bucket with a plastic lid that sealed airtight. The gas pellets should have done their sterilization trick by now.

She picked up the bucket, opened it and pulled out his badge and then his gun with her thumb and forefinger. "If we're going to be partners, Clint, then I guess you should have these."

"Thank you."

The corners of his mouth crinkled a fraction as he took them.

She took that as a Texas Ranger smile.

Yesterday's sunshine and blue skies were gone. As Clint followed Macy's lead into the woods, titanium clouds weighed as heavily on his shoulders as his mood. He was grateful to her for giving his gun and badge back. For reminding him he was still a Ranger, if only for another day. For as long as he carried it, he had a duty to the badge. A duty to the people of the state that gave it to him.

He had no business letting himself be distracted by a woman.

The problem was, as surely as Macy had reminded him he was still a Ranger, she had also reminded him he was still a man. It had been a long time since he'd even noticed a woman, much less thought of one as anything more serious than an entertaining way to spend an evening, or let off a little steam.

But Macy Attois had gotten deeper under his skin

than most. She had him wanting to do outrageous things just to see her warm coffee eyes widen in surprise. Wanting to protect her from any and all comers, microscopic or otherwise.

If he really wanted to protect her, he'd leave her the hell alone. She had enough on her plate without adding a down-on-his-luck, soon-to-be-ex-Ranger.

He actually considered warning her off. Telling her he was damaged goods. That he wouldn't be a Ranger, wasn't sure he'd be much of anything, once this nightmare was over, the monkey caught or found dead, and he got back to Dallas so he could sign his resignation. Trouble was, he suspected telling her would only draw her to him more.

Big-hearted as she was, he'd bet she couldn't pass by a three-legged dog on the side of the highway, either, without stopping to pick it up.

His bad shoulder aching, he straightened up and leaned on the machete he'd been swinging. The underbrush was nearly impenetrable in this part of the forest. The going had been slow, as they'd taken meticulous care through the gauntlet of thorns and trip vines, knowing their furry little friend could be waiting for them on the next tree limb or behind the next tangle of scrub.

"How much farther to the next trap?" he asked, wishing he could mop the sweat off his forehead. With the clouds had come an almost stifling rise in the humidity.

He settled for sliding the CDC supply pack that carried the basics—water, first-aid kit, flashlights—off his back and rolling his neck to work the kinks out.

Macy frowned at her GPS. "About three hundred yards."

He suppressed a groan. Might as well have been three hundred miles, as thick as it was out here. They'd set out shortly after eight this morning, yet it had been nearly noon before they'd reached their first set of assigned co-ordinates to find an empty trap. After that they'd hit about one an hour. Of the four they'd checked, two had been empty. One contained a seriously pissed-off possum and the last was in several mangled pieces. Clint wasn't sure if it had been broken when it was dropped from the hel-icopter, or some critter had smashed it for the food inside.

A javelina could do that. The wild pigs had been known to raid campgrounds and leave nothing behind in one piece, including the campers.

Macy peered upward through the boughs overhead. "It's going to rain, isn't it?"

"Yep."

Her sigh cut straight through him. "José was raised in captivity. I don't know what he'll do if he's caught out in a storm."

"You're worried about the *monkey?*"

"I'm worried about *catching* the monkey. Whether he decides to hole up and ride it out, or panics and makes a mad dash for who-knows-where, it makes it harder for us to find him."

Of course. He should have realized that.

"We'd best get back at it, then." He hefted the ma-chete over his shoulder and made a hacking cut at the wall of growth before them. "Maybe we'll get lucky and find him before we all get drenched."

They didn't.

The thunder rolled in first, then the wind turned

around out of the north, bringing a chill and kicking up bits of leaves and dirt. When the rain finally came, it came in sheets. The pitiful ponchos included in their supply packs did little to protect them. They were soaked to the skin and shivering within seconds.

Reaching back to help Macy over a rotted tree trunk downed in their path, Clint thought he felt her shiver. It was hard to tell for sure, since he couldn't see anything of her except a blurry swash of color. Apparently they didn't make gas masks with windshield wipers.

"We need to find some cover," he shouted over the drumming rain.

She shook her head and passed him by. "We need to keep going."

But even as she said it, she stopped. She swayed slightly, then took a step back. Clint leaned around her shoulder to see a twenty-foot ravine so steep it might have been the edge of the world. A rush of runoff water careened through the bottom of the gorge, twirling broken limbs and clumps of debris in its currents.

"Great," he said.

"How do we get across that?"

He wished he had an answer for her. "You wait here. I'll scout out a crossing."

"No, wait." He had already turned to leave. She reached out for his arm. "We should stay togeth—"

She tripped over a low vine and the ground beneath her feet gave way. As if it was happening in slow motion, Clint saw her arms flail, her legs shoot out from under her.

Then a flash of lightning blinded him. He yelled, but the thunder obliterated the sound.

Wildly, he grabbed for her. Caught a bit of cloth, then lost it. Felt an elbow scrape by his palm. And finally latched on to one thin wrist.

Concentrating on the feel of each fragile bone crushed in his grip and not letting go, he opened his eyes and found that some time in the last half second, he had landed on his belly in the mud. He lay at an angle toward the ravine, his legs pointed more or less toward safe territory, his whole right shoulder dangling over the precipice.

In between gusts of wind and the splatter of rain against his face shield, he could hear Macy's terrified gulps of air. He tried to snake backward, to pull her up, but he couldn't get enough purchase on the slippery bank.

"Hang on," he told her. Ordered her. Demanded her. "Goddamn it, you hang on!"

But her hand was small. Her fingers weren't even long enough to reach all the way up around his wrist in a solid grip.

And his hand…his hand was trembling.

He tried to stop it. He begged. He pleaded to God to stop it.

And then he watched helplessly as she slid out of his weakened grasp and tumbled over the rocks and roots into the water below.

Macy's hip collided with something hard and sharp. Her foot caught in something momentarily while her body continued to tumble forward, sending her flying facedown toward the foaming white water below. The

GPS she'd been holding slipped away, shattered on a rock. Macy held her breath, knowing she was about to hit bottom.

Cold, dark water closed over her head. Entombed her. She fought the instinct to gasp, to breathe. She had to wait. Wait until she bobbed back to the surface.

But her clothes were heavy. They weighed her down. Her boots had already filled with water. She could feel the liquid pressure against her face mask. The seal wouldn't hold. It wasn't made for swimming.

With panic shooting streams of fire into her veins, she fought the coldness. The dark. She kicked her legs. Kicked her boots off. Waved her arms, hoping she was propelling herself in the right direction. Looking for light, she turned her head, and her temple struck a heavy limb. Her mask slipped sideways, then was swept away. The current grabbed her, too, pulling her down and under. She grabbed the limb, which wasn't floating, but wedged against the bank somehow, and followed it to the surface, climbing it like it was a live tree.

She'd probably only been underwater for seconds before she surfaced, but she coughed and sputtered all the same. She tasted brackish water. Her arms and legs were numb.

Teeth chattering, she looked back upstream to see what had happened to Clint, but he was nowhere in sight. How far had the current carried her?

It didn't matter. He would find her sooner or later. Right now she had to get out of this water.

Cautiously she edged along the tree limb toward the bank. It was too steep for her to climb, but maybe Clint

could lower something down to her, pull her out when
he found her.

She'd pulled herself along about half of the five-foot
tree limb when her knee bumped something hung up on
one of the smaller branches below the surface. A piece
of white material billowed in the current. Macy reached
out to push the debris out of her way, and the something
turned. A human face stared up at her out of the water.

A face with a neat, round bullet hole in the center of
the forehead.

Chapter 8

"Macy? Macy!"

Macy's silence had Clint crashing heedlessly through the underbrush along the top of the ravine, trying to get a glimpse of her. Her scream froze him in his muddy tracks.

It wasn't a scream of pain, but one of terror.

What the hell?

The monkey. It had to be. God, she'd stumbled right on the infected monkey. Or it had stumbled on her.

"Macy!"

A new surge of adrenaline lit his blood on fire. He jumped a fallen log, skidded on his heels over a rock covered with lichen, and sailed over the edge of the ravine without pause when he caught a glimpse of her in the water below.

He grabbed an exposed root and used it to slow his slide, then bumped down the rest of the slope on his heels and his butt to find himself standing in hip-deep water next to a dead man.

"Are you all right?" he asked Macy.

She nodded, but her teeth were chattering. A knot of fear hardened in his gut when he realized she'd lost her bio mask.

"It—it's Michael," she said.

"Michael who?"

"Mike Cain. Our pilot. He's been shot."

And he was a long way from the plane crash. Even the biggest, most desperate coyote wouldn't have dragged him this far.

Which meant either the pilot had been shot and thrown out of the plane before it went down, or had survived the crash and walked into the woods before being shot.

What the hell was he doing? He didn't have time for this now. He had to get Macy out of here.

He heaved the pilot to the wide end of the fallen tree, closest to shore, and hooked him over a sturdy limb where he wouldn't be washed away, and then swept Macy into his arms. She felt small as a child, cradled against his chest, but there was nothing childlike about the plush curves that nestled against his body, or the wave of protectiveness, so fierce it was almost animalistic, that washed up inside him.

"What are you doing?" she asked, squirming against him.

Knowing she had to be freezing, he pulled her closer to his body heat. "We've got to get out of here."

"But Michael—"

"Nothing we can do to help him. We'll send some-one back later."

She opened her mouth to argue, but he wasn't listening. He was moving.

Trying to climb the muddy bank here was useless, so he waded downstream to a spot where it wasn't so steep.

When he got her on dry land—figuratively speaking—he set her on a large, flat rock and ran his hands up and down her arms and legs, feeling for broken bones, signs of blood or other injury.

"Are you sure you're okay? Do you hurt anywhere?"

"I'm fine. Ow!" She grimaced as he probed her ankle. He immediately gentled his touch, his chest tightening with concern.

"Okay, I'm not fine. But I'll live. I just twisted it, I think. It caught on something when I was falling."

"It's starting to swell already. You're not going to be able to walk out of here."

Her gaze roamed the trees on all sides. "To be honest, without my bio mask, I wouldn't want to try."

Christ, the monkey. The virus. She had no protection.

She wrapped her arms around herself and squeezed. Her gaze darted left and then right. "Do you think who-ever shot him is still out here?"

"I doubt it. From the looks of him, he'd been dead awhile."

"Do—" A shudder racked her shoulders. "Do you think he could come back?"

Clint's jaw went hard. He didn't think so, but

stranger things had happened. "We're not waiting around to find out. Give me the satellite phone, we'll call for a chopper to come pick you up."

She reached into the pouch at her waist. Her hand came back empty. She didn't have to tell him what had happened to it. It was somewhere at the bottom of the creek.

Terror rose in her in palpable waves. What little color had been left in her cheeks paled. Her eyes rounded to huge, dark, sunken saucers set in an alabaster face.

"It's all right," he told her. But it wasn't. There was an infected monkey and possibly a gunman and God knew what else out here.

With a growl, he ripped his mask off and lifted it toward her head. The monkey, at least, he could protect her from.

"What are you doing?" She shoved his hands away. "Clint, no. Put that back on."

He clamped one hand around both her wrists. She jerked and wriggled, trying to pull away. "Don't fight me."

"If the monkey is in this area, I've already been infected."

"And if he's not, I plan to make sure he doesn't get another chance."

"By giving up your own protection?"

She managed to get one hand free and lurched away from him. He pulled her back by the other hand and braced her back against his chest. Their hearts pounded each other like two rams butting heads.

"You're a doctor," he said, struggling for some semblance of calm.

"And that makes my life more important than yours? You're a Texas Ranger, for God's sake. You don't think that's worth something?"

The sickness that had been festering in his gut for weeks spread to his mind, his heart. This was his fault. He couldn't hold her. Hadn't been able to pull a hundred-and-ten-pound woman to safety when her life depended on it.

So what was his life worth now?

"Not as much as it used to be."

Barely holding back a growl of guilty frustration, he yanked his biohazard mask over her head and checked to make sure each strap was tight as she watched him through wounded eyes.

She didn't understand. How could she? And he wasn't about to explain.

Not as much as it goddamn used to be.

"It's miles back to camp. You can't carry me the whole way." Macy's face shield bumped the back of Clint's head as he slipped in the mud, righted himself. She'd been riding him piggyback-style for a good twenty minutes. He was breathing hard, but showed no signs of slowing.

"We're not going back to camp," he said.

Her arms tightened around his shoulders. The woods on all sides seemed deeper and darker, more dangerous than ever. "Then where are we going?"

They needed to get back to camp, where it was safe. Where he wouldn't risk sucking in death with each labored breath he drew.

She hadn't been able to convince him to take back his mask, the jerk, and it wasn't like she could throw him to the ground and force it on him.

"Back to the last trap we checked," he huffed. "I think there's a place there we can hole up until we can get some help."

It was a fire tower, he explained when they were close enough to see the metal stilts rising through the tops of the trees. The Forestry Service used to use them as observation posts during fire season, but they were mostly abandoned now. Clint had seen this one a couple-dozen yards away from the last trap they'd checked.

He set her down at the base.

She peered up, but couldn't see what sat atop the stilts for the trees in the way. "How do we get up there?"

Clint walked around, his head also turned upward. "There should be a ladder. There it is." He pointed.

It was a retractable type, like the ones on fire escapes. Probably to keep unauthorized people, like them, from climbing the tower. A metal box housed the pulley system that would lower the steps. Clint used the butt of his gun to whack off the rusted lock.

"Here we go," he said as the ladder creaked down. "Can you climb?"

"I'll dance the rumba if it means getting somewhere dry." Somewhere far above sick monkeys and floating corpses. She shivered, wrapped her arms around herself. "Please tell me this thing has a roof."

"This thing has a roof."

"Thank the Lord."

He put her on the ladder before him and followed her

up, his feet just one rung lower than hers, his body behind her, shielding her and bracing her. Ready to catch her if she fell.

The seventy-five-foot climb was slow and painful. The steps of the ladder were slippery and her ankle ached. By the time she reached the four-by-four square shack perched far above the treetops, it was all Macy could do to drag herself inside and flop onto her back, spread-eagled. Or as close to spread-eagled as a girl could get in a four-foot-square room.

The Ranger pulled himself in after her and shook his head like a dog, splattering water across all four walls, then leaned into the small, square hole cut in the wall that looked out over the forest to the west. "I think we'll be pretty safe up here. Come see."

Macy couldn't summon the energy to move, much less get up and look out the window. She did manage to pull off her face mask. It felt good to breathe unfiltered air again. She inhaled deeply, smelling the forest and the rain. "The virus shouldn't drift this high."

He pulled the rope and retracted the ladder. "I hope José won't be able to pay us an unexpected visit, either."

"He could probably shinny up the stilts, but I doubt he'd climb a metal structure when he's got all those trees to play in down there."

"All right, then." The Ranger rubbed his hands together. She watched him through heavy eyelids. "That takes care of shelter."

Of course, now that they had a roof over their heads, the rain had stopped. Only the occasional stray drop pinged on the tin overhead.

"Let's see what we can do about the other necessities." He dug through his pack, pulling out and inspecting items. "Water. Bananas."

"Those are for the traps."

"Not anymore. First-aid kit. Disinfectant." He opened the lid on the bottle of antibacterial gel, squeezed some out in his palm and then tossed the bottle to her before slathering his hands together. "Scrub down," he said and then kept digging in the pack.

"Here we go. Survival blankets." He tore open the plastic pack, unfolded the crinkly silver sheet and handed it to her. "Not exactly a down comforter, but it'll conserve at least a little body heat. Take those wet coveralls off."

That woke her up. "In your dreams."

His hands went still. He turned his head toward her. Shadows and whisker stubs darkened his face, but his eyes were fever-bright. "If this were my dream, honey, you wouldn't have to take them off. I'd do it for you."

Macy clamped her teeth together to keep her jaw from dropping.

"Come on. Rain poncho first." He waggled his fingers at her. "Give it to me."

The poncho was uncomfortable. It kept tangling up her arms. She pulled herself into a sitting position, her back propped against the wall, and dragged it over her head.

"Good girl," he said when she handed the tattered yellow vinyl to him.

He yanked his poncho off and tied the two together, then put his butt on the windowsill and levered his shoulders through the hole. A moment later, he disappeared through the opening altogether.

"Are you crazy? You're going to fall!"

"I hope not. It's a long way down."

She scooted to the window, looked up and saw the toes of his rubber boots perched on a strip of metal about as wide as an elementary school ruler. "What are you doing up there?"

"Making a distress flag, I hope. When we don't show up at camp by nightfall, they're bound to send choppers out looking for us first thing in the morning. This bright yellow ought to be visible from a good distance."

"Oh." Pretty clever, her Ranger.

Not too smart, giving up his bio mask with a lethal virus floating around, but definitely clever.

And when had he become *her* Ranger?

"Are you naked yet?" he called out as casually as if he'd been ordering a burger and fries at the drive-through, and she realized he was trying to make a joke of it, to relieve a little of the anxiety in the situation, even if his humor did sound a little forced.

She appreciated the effort, but she really wasn't in a laughing mood. She was tired and cold. She was sad for the lives that had been lost, worried for those that might yet be lost, including his, and she was scared.

Scared that the searchers wouldn't find them in the morning. Scared that when she closed her eyes tonight, she'd see monkeys swinging through the trees, just out of reach, and corpses floating in the creeks and rivers.

Scared that she was going to be spending the night

on the cramped floor of a tiny room with a very large man, and only a scrap of silver blanket to separate them.

Scared that maybe she wished there were nothing to separate them at all.

Clint hooked his feet back into the window, grabbed on to the edge of the roof and swung himself into the room, nearly landing on top of Macy. She was huddled in the corner, the silver blanket tucked up to her chin. She'd unbraided her hair, and the wet, heavy waves fell around her shoulders like an auburn shawl.

Their gazes met, then his slid down. Past the edge of the blanket to the floor. To the puddle of blue coveralls against the far wall.

The hairs on the back of his neck stood up as if there were another storm moving in. Tension crackled and popped in the room. Heat suffused his body from the toes up.

At least he wasn't shivering any longer.

"Your turn," she said, and the sound of her voice pulled his gaze back to hers. Her eyes were still wide. Shocked.

He looked away, studied the floor. "You know, I didn't much care for this jumpsuit when your people issued it to me after decon."

"And your point is?"

He risked a quick glance at her, tried to communicate with a look what he couldn't with words: regret. "It's starting to grow on me."

"Chicken."

"Damn straight." He jammed his fingers into his

pockets, leaned his hips against the wall across from her. As far away as he could get. "Look, Macy. You've had a hell of a day. We both have."

"Your point, again?"

"Stress and naked bodies don't mix well."

"Afraid I'm going to seduce you, Clint?" she asked softly. Dark was falling outside. Only the thin light of the sun setting behind the clouds gave the tower room a soft, shadowed glow.

"I'm afraid you won't have to," he answered honestly.

His life was coming apart at the seams. How easy it would be to forget his troubles in her. The sight of her. The scent. The warm, wet heat.

She deserved better.

He turned to stare out the window. Mist clung to the dark treetops, pooling in spots like filmy lakes. The sun's last rays set the lakes aglow. The moon had already risen in a clear sky above it all.

The rustle of plastic warned him she was coming before he felt Macy behind him.

"It's beautiful," she said, looking over his shoulder.

Not as beautiful as her.

He faced her and couldn't resist tucking a strand of dark, wavy hair behind her ear while she studied him with luminous eyes.

"I don't want to hurt you," he breathed.

"I don't want to be hurt." The warmth of her hands seeped through the damp coveralls where she laid her palms on his chest. "But I would like to be held."

She let him decide. He liked that about her. It

wouldn't have taken much to push him over the edge. A kiss. A touch. But she stood back and let him decide.

In the end, she didn't have to push him over the edge.

He leapt willingly.

Macy sighed against Clint's lips when he leaned down to kiss her. She let the blanket fall when he banded his strong arms around her.

He'd made his decision. He told her so with his kneading fingers on her shoulders, her back. His teeth on her lips, nibbling possessively, his tongue, teasing.

Tentatively, she reached up, framed his jaw with her hands. His whiskers were rough. Arousing. She traced his ears with her fingertips, ducked her head to suck on the hollow of his throat.

Moaning, he turned her until her back was against the wall. The slight impact of her back against the cool metal had the breath shooting out of her. The feel of Clint's hand circling her breast had her dragging in another lungful.

"You like that, baby?" he murmured against her ear.

She nodded silently, incapable of speech.

"How about this?" He lowered his head, laved the valley between her breasts with his tongue, and then pulled her nipple into his mouth.

"Oh, God!"

She should have known he would possess the same mute intensity in lovemaking that he displayed in other matters. She could feel the tension building in him, simmering, yet none of what he felt showed on his face. No urgent words of need escaped his lips. He searched out and exploited every sensitive spot on her body one at a time, hardly giving her time to catch her breath before moving on to the next.

Bonelessly, she slumped to the floor and he came down on top of her, shedding his wet jumpsuit as he went. She writhed beneath him, luxuriating in the friction of his body on hers. The hard muscle holding her in place. The velvet-soft skin over the steely erection brushing her thigh.

She reached for it, but he sensed her intent, pulled his hips away and gave her his fingers instead. Inside her. Stretching her and lubricating her. She clamped her hand over his and pushed him deeper. Faster.

"Easy, baby," he rumbled, the tip of her breast still in his mouth, but she didn't hear.

She was lost in sensation. Desperate.

She'd never felt like this with another man. She enjoyed sex, but she'd never needed it. Never craved it the way she did now.

"Please," she whispered, knowing he would understand what she was asking for. Hoping he would give it to her.

As if her wishes had made it come true, he inserted another finger, stroked her twice more and then pressed his thumb against the cluster of nerves that formed the center of her world at that moment.

Her back arched. Her hips drove up, into his hand. Her body became a vortex and all of her blood, her consciousness swirled to that one spot, circled on the edge of oblivion for one long second, and then dropped.

Her stomach plummeted. Her muscles clenched in a

spasm so strong she had to grind her teeth to keep herself from screaming. Bright light blinded her, then faded slowly to gray.

In the darkness, she could just make out Clint's silhouette above her. His forehead was furrowed.

"You needed that," he said.

She tried to laugh, but it came out a warble. "Who doesn't need that?"

He pushed the damp hair off her forehead, frowning. "It's been a long time for you."

"Since I felt like that? How about since, oh…never?"

She felt his hesitation, his resignation. "David didn't—"

"David was kind. And smart. Ambitious as a man could be. But he had a hard time finding his keys in the morning, much less my—"

"I get the picture."

"I sound so awful, criticizing him when he's dead, and I'm alive."

"Too many people idealize the dead. It's better just to tell the truth."

Tears stung her eyes. The truth was, she didn't want to talk about David. Not while she lay in another man's arms.

"Will you tell me the truth, Clint?"

"I'll try."

It was full dark now. He was just a voice in the darkness. It made it easier to ask. "Do you feel anything. Here." She traced a finger through the springy curls of his chest hair to a spot just above his heart. "Down deep. Do you laugh? Do you cry? Do you ever just get really, really mad?"

She knew instantly that she'd said the wrong thing. His back stiffened. "I'm not a damned robot."

He rolled away. Sorry she'd asked, sorry she'd doubted him, she grabbed on and rolled with him, ending up with him on his back on the floor and her on top.

His hands came up to move her aside, but she locked her fingers around his wrists and pushed them over his head. His chest heaved between her legs.

She stared down at him a long time, trying to make out his features. The broken nose. The dent in his chin. The eyes that glowed faintly even in the absence of light.

"What does it take to break your discipline?" she wondered out loud. "To make you lose control?"

She still had his arms pinned to the floor. His fists clenched rhythmically, but he didn't struggle. "Why don't you try to find out?"

A small smile stole across her lips. Could he see it in the dark?

"I think I'll do that."

Letting go of his wrists, she shimmied down his body, grazing her hands in serpentines over his shoulders, his chest, his abdomen as she went. His stomach muscles fluttered. His erection twitched against her bottom.

She leaned over to delve her tongue in his navel and lifted her hips, then sank down on his shaft an inch at a time. Undulating, lifting, delving, sinking. Lifting. Sinking.

His arms jerked up. His fingers dug into her hips, urging her on as she seated herself fully on him, then leaned back and rode.

His breathing grew short and ragged. She quickened her rocking to keep pace. Then she slowed and clenched her muscles around him and he bucked.

"Oh, baby. Don't stop. Don't stop."

She couldn't have if she'd wanted to. Her own need was flying up, up again, as if he were a horse with wings, carrying her into the clouds. Into the stratosphere.

She was ready to explode, but she bit her lip, holding on, determined to make him lose control first.

She leaned back and pulled his knees up, wrapped her arms around his thighs and concentrated on pumping harder. Taking him deeper. She arched her back and tilted her hips, plunged down on him and raised herself up, then fell again.

A cry escaped her. She couldn't hold herself together much longer.

Then Clint growled. His back came off the floor. His hands shook as he lifted her, flipped her and came down on her with crushing force and she smiled inside because she knew at that moment, he had no control. No discipline.

He thrust against her one more time. Twice. And when his back stiffened and he called out her name, there was no hiding the truth. No hiding his feelings.

He was as desperate, and as transparent, as she.

Chapter 9

Straddling the roof of the fire tower, Clint guided the winch with the safety harness and little round seat dangling at the end toward the window below, where Macy waited to strap herself in. They'd woken to the chop of helicopter rotors. The search team had spotted the bright yellow ponchos he'd tied out almost as soon as they'd taken off.

Their arrival had preempted the obligatory morning-after talk. He hadn't been looking forward to it, but to be honest, he had some things that needed to be said, uncomfortable or not.

She was the kind of woman who would be likely to have expectations after a night like they'd shared. Hopes for the future.

He needed to let her know that that wasn't an option

for him right now. Not when he didn't know what kind of future he had to offer her.

Who was he kidding? It wouldn't matter even if his future was all mapped out with a one-hundred-percent guarantee.

Clint just didn't do women like Macy Attois. Women who loved more deeply than he would ever be capable of loving them back.

Yeah, sooner or later, they were going to have to have that talk.

The winch operator on the helicopter hovering above was making frantic hand signals at him. Clint looked down and saw Macy hanging half in, half out of the fire-tower window, strapped on to the seat with her legs wrapped around the dangling cable.

His body temperature rose a couple of degrees remembering what it had felt like to have those legs locked around him last night, then he pushed the thought away for later.

Once she'd been hoisted into the chopper, it was his turn. It was a wild ride, spinning and wind-blown, as was the short trip back to base camp.

On the ground, blood tests were dispensed with first. He and Macy had essentially been quarantined in the fire tower for more than the requisite twelve hours, so they didn't have to wait long for the results.

Negative.

They'd been lucky. Again.

The camp was busy. He saw some of the Hempaxe crew coming and going with their CDC partners. Security personnel were on constant lookout around the perimeter. Supplies were being unloaded. Maps were being pointed at by planning crews, lines drawn, routes plotted. Someone had cleared enough of a trail to get four-wheel ATVs in to them, and a motor hummed as someone revved one of them up.

Macy went off with her team to get a status update. A young man whose bio mask looked out of place with his state trooper's uniform called to Clint. "Are you Ranger Sergeant Hayes?"

The "yes" that once would have tumbled easily out of his mouth nearly choked him. After yesterday, he needed to think seriously about his ability to perform as a ranger even in this limited capacity. He'd put Macy at risk, and that was inexcusable.

He took the phone. Captain Matheson's voice boomed in his ear. "You're supposed to be keeping things under control out there, Hayes, not going off on safari."

"Yeah, well, Tarzan always was my hero."

"So tell me about this DB that Jane found."

The Dead Body. Mystery of the day. "Male, Caucasian, midforties. One small-caliber bullet hole in the forehead. Dr. Attois identified him as the pilot of the plane, Michael Cain. Twenty years in the air force, two years in the Gulf. Solid record, according to the military. Went to work for the CDC after he retired."

"Was he shot before or after the crash?"

"After, I suspect, but you'll have to ask the Medical Examiner to be sure."

Bull blew out a hard breath. "So at least one man survived the crash."

"Two," Clint said, automatically looking around to see who might be in listening range. "Michael Cain. And whoever killed him."

"Injuries consistent with a fall from an aircraft?"

"Not that I could see."

"You thinking what I'm thinking?"

"I'm thinking maybe the accident was more than just an accident."

"That's what I'm thinking. Attempted hijacking, maybe?"

"Somebody wanted the virus? The damn bug is running rampant in Malaysia. You'd think they could have gotten all they wanted without having to steal a plane."

"We don't have all the pieces yet. But something happened up there that wasn't supposed to."

Clint could practically hear Bull Matheson turning the puzzle over in his mind, viewing it from all angles.

"Clint, Dr. Attois's fiancé was on the flight, right?"

"Ex-fiancé."

"And she flew home commercial?"

Clint's hand tightened on the satellite phone. "She's not involved."

"They could have been working together. Her going home first to set things up."

"Why would they want ARFIS?"

"Like I said, we don't have all the pieces."

"Like *I* said. She's not involved."

"That doesn't sound like the clear-headed, uninvolved investigator I know and love speaking."

Clint ground his teeth. If he gripped the phone any harder, he was afraid he'd crush it. "What do you want?"

"You have a relationship with her, I assume."

Clint neither confirmed nor denied. Relationship could cover a lot of ground. Friends. Acquaintances. Lovers.

"Use it," the captain finished. "Find out what she knows."

Clint said goodbye and hung up. Across the camp, Macy walked out of her tent, and looked his way. He couldn't see much of her face behind the bio mask, but he'd bet his last paycheck that she'd pulled her lower lip between her teeth and smiled shyly, pausing a moment as she remembered last night. He nodded stiffly in acknowledgement.

Looked like he'd be having that morning-after talk with her sooner rather than later. At least when it was over he wouldn't have to worry about her having expectations of him. Not after he accused her of murder.

Macy was in her tent with her sore ankle propped up on a chair when Clint walked in, balancing two lunch trays on one arm. She'd never been much on fussing over her looks with makeup, but just this once she wished she'd bothered to put on a little lipstick and do more with her wild hair than pull it back in a quick braid.

"One of those for me?" she asked, nodding at his cargo, "or are you making up for missing dinner last night?"

"You can have turkey on white or turkey on white."

She smiled. "Turkey on white is fine. Thanks."

He passed her a tray and she unwrapped the cellophane around her sandwich. Her stomach did a somersault when she thought about taking a bite, so she set it down.

"Did they—have they sent someone out to get Michael yet?"

He nodded.

"Who could have shot him? And why?"

Uncharacteristically, he studied his tray instead of meeting her eyes. The change in his behavior made her nervous. What was going on?

"You tell me," he said.

"What do you mean?"

"Can you think of any reason someone would want to kill your pilot?"

Her stomach progressed from somersaults to full handsprings. She pushed her lunch tray away. "No."

"What about the cargo guy, Jeffries? Or David?"

"No one would have any reason to kill them, either."

"I meant would they have any reason to kill Michael Cain."

She lurched to her feet. "No!"

Clint calmly took a bite of his sandwich and chewed in silence. She pushed her chair back and limped across the tent, her mind racing.

"Are you interrogating me?" she asked, spinning back to face him.

He looked up, took his time swallowing. "I'm trying to figure out what happened out there. It's what I do."

She hobbled back over to him, plopped into her seat. "I didn't know Ty very well. But David did not shoot Michael. And if you're even considering the possibility that he did, that means…you think he's alive."

Her heart stuttered. He did. Clint thought David was alive!

"Don't get ahead of yourself," he said. "We don't know what's going on here. Can you think of any reason someone would want to get their hands on the virus the plane was carrying. Could terrorists use it somehow?"

It was hard to put her hope that David might be alive aside and think about the virus, but she tried. "They could, but they'd be stupid to do it. The only reason it's been contained in Malaysia so far is because it's a small country, easy to close the borders. But if ARFIS were released in the U.S. or Europe, they'd be risking a worldwide outbreak. They'd be jeopardizing their own countries."

"What kind of knowledge would it take to handle the virus without contaminating yourself if someone did take it?"

"Your average high-school science teacher could probably thaw the frozen virus and weaponize it."

"Wonderful. And the instructions to make an atomic bomb are posted on the Internet. Ain't it a wonderful world we live in?"

"If you knew David, you'd never think he was involved in some terrorist plot to kill God knows how many innocent people."

Clint took another bite of his lunch and scooted her tray closer to her, giving her an encouraging look. "You need to eat. Tell me about Ty Jeffries. He's the wild card here. Foreign national, you hadn't known him that long."

She picked up her sandwich, nibbled at the crust and shrugged. "We called him the red-tape man. He purchased supplies for us, acquired the test animals, arranged for shipping, dealt with the airport authorities, stuff like that. Maintained most of our equipment, too. He was very handy. David and I are...not mechanical."

"Why was he going back to the U.S.?"

"David liked him. Offered him a job."

"What kind of background checks do you do on employees?"

"Extensive. Although Ty wasn't an employee yet. He was working as a contractor for us in Malaysia."

"So you basically let a man you know nothing about on board a plane carrying a lethal virus."

"David—" She ducked her head. She would not blame this on David. Not without him here to defend himself.

"David what?"

She lifted her head. "Nothing. I guess you're right. We screwed up."

"Had David ever hired anyone from a field mission before?"

"Not that I know of."

"Could he have been under any coercion this time?"

"You mean Ty forced David to bring him on that plane?"

He took a long drink from a bottle of water. "Or bribed him. Offered him something he couldn't resist?"

Macy's nerves sizzled. Clint had struck a sore spot. If David had one weakness, it was his ambition. "No."

Clint looked up as if he'd heard the lie in her voice.

"Why did you really break off your engagement to him?"

She jerked as if he'd slapped her. She waited for his expression to soften. For him to apologize.

She should have known better. He sat there stone-faced.

"None of your damned business." She tried to get up, but he stopped her by clamping his hand over her wrist. "Let me go."

"Did you know he was up to something? Is that what you fought about before you gave his ring back?"

Her eyes stung. "We didn't fight. I just—I couldn't be with him anymore."

"Because he wouldn't cut you in on whatever he'd gotten into."

"Because I didn't love him!"

He leaned forward in his chair, pulled her closer to him. Storm clouds brewed dangerously in his pewter eyes. "Or maybe he was just your patsy, and you were through with him. Did you sleep your way close to ARFIS, to the connection with Ty? Maybe you're the one working with Jeffries. After all, David wasn't even supposed to be on that plane."

"Bastard!" She jerked her arm out of his grasp—or maybe he let her go, she didn't know which, didn't care. All she cared about was getting out of there.

Slowing down only long enough to don her protective gear, she stormed out of the tent without looking back.

Macy shuffled across the compound as fast as she could with one good leg. The rain and the foot traffic had turned the grassy meadow into a bog that could suck a girl's boots off if she weren't careful.

With each slurping step she alternated between wounded feelings and fury.

How could he?

How dare he?

How could he?

Who did he think he was, accusing David of using ARFIS for his own gain? Accusing her?

But even as her heart ached that he didn't trust her, and her mind railed at his unfounded accusations of David, her mind turned over the facts. The plane had crashed. Someone had shot the pilot. People were missing. ARFIS, in the wrong hands, could make Europe's bubonic plague epidemic of the Middle Ages look like a preschool chicken-pox outbreak.

And David…David had been acting strangely those last few days.

She'd thought he'd just been tired. Maybe sensing her unhappiness with their relationship.

Had it been more?

She heard her name and turned to wait for Susan, who was waddling determinedly through the muck in her direction.

"Macy," she called looking down at the clipboard in her hands as she walked. "We ran another set of tests on the—"

Susan glanced up. Her eyes widened. Her mouth pursed. "What's wrong? Oh, no. Not the virus. Your blood work was fine. I checked it myself."

"I don't have ARFIS."

Just then Clint stepped out of her tent and walked across the compound to talk to Skip Hollister, who was in from checking traps.

Susan's eyes narrowed. "What did he do to you?"

"Nothing." Macy knew she didn't lie well. She kicked at a clod of dirt. "You worked a lot with David those last few days in Malaysia. Did he seem…normal to you?"

She laughed. "Dr. Brinker, normal? Never."

"I mean, did he act differently? Give any indication that something might be wrong?"

"Well, you know how it is on field missions. And this one was worse than most. We work all kinds of crazy hours, and you hear things."

"What kind of things?"

Susan's cheeks turned rosy behind her face shield. "I heard about the two of you splitting up. Never was sure what you saw in him, anyway. He was a little more jittery than normal. I figured he was upset, but trying to, you know, cover it up."

"Did he say he was upset?"

"No." She gave Macy a sympathetic look. "He was just really distracted. Is something wrong, Dr. Attois? I mean, everything's wrong, with the plane crash, and José loose, but…is something else going on?"

"I don't know." Macy watched Clint disappear into the security tent with Skip.

But I darned sure plan to find out.

Chapter 10

Christian and Curtis, Macy's logistics guy and her second lab tech, ran a squeeze play on Clint in the chow line the next morning. They pinned him right between the butter beans and the fried chicken. The food had gotten better in the last twenty-four hours. Seems the women in town found out there were some government men in the woods searching for the "rabid" monkey and they insisted on bringing casseroles and pies—not to mention fried chicken—to sustain the hearty hunters protecting their town.

Curtis and Christian certainly seemed to approve of the country hospitality. Their trays were loaded.

Curtis kept a lookout, probably watching for Macy, while Christian started the proceedings. The intimidation proceedings, that was.

"Been hearing some trash talk about you and Dr. At-tois," Christian said. He was young, but not a kid. He'd probably seen the top side of thirty a year or two ago.

"That so," Clint said noncommittally.

Curtis glanced over his shoulder. "She's been upset ever since you got back from checking traps yester-day."

"She say what she was upset about?"

"She didn't have to," Christian said. "Macy's not real good at hiding what she's feeling."

"Yeah, I noticed that." So, apparently, had every-one else.

"She was on the rebound, man," Curtis said more ve-hemently. "You had to know that. She was trying to get her head straight. She didn't need somebody coming along messing her up again."

Clint didn't have a comeback for that one. Some-times a man just had to take his lumps.

"My sister said that ever since Macy talked to you, she's been asking all kinds of questions about Dr. Brinker and Ty Jeffries."

"Has she now?" *Interesting. Doing a little investigating on your own, are you, doc?*

"She even asked me if I thought David could have been seeing someone else."

"Was he?"

Christian snorted. "David? Hell, no. He was more in-terested in laboratory mice than women. Well, except for Macy. And even she took second seat sometimes."

"We heard she found the pilot in the woods and that he'd been shot," Christian said.

Curtis added, "We want to know what's up with that. And what you intend to do about Macy."

Clint inched down the line past the chicken and grabbed himself a dinner roll. His two shadows followed.

"What's up," he said quietly, not wanting to announce it to the whole camp. "Is that we're investigating Michael's death. And that's all I'm going to tell you about an open case."

Curtis added two rolls to the mountain on his tray. "He was murdered for real, then?"

"For real."

"Whoa."

Clint turned to walk away. Christian followed, swung around in front of him, cutting him off. "And what about the other?"

"What other?"

"What you're going to do about Macy."

He'd said sometimes a man had to take his lumps, but some lumps were a lot bigger than others. This one was about the size of Mount Everest. The last thing he'd ever wanted to do was hurt her, and yet he had. So badly that even her staff noticed.

What the hell had he been trying to prove?

In his own stupid way, he supposed he'd been trying to prove her innocence. He'd needed to make the accusations, see her reactions. She wouldn't be able to keep the truth from him. Everything in her heart showed on her face. Everything.

Including the hurt. The pain of the betrayal she'd felt with each ugly insinuation he'd thrown at her.

At the time, he'd thought it was better this way.

"I'll talk to her," he promised, and his stomach rolled even as he spoke. What could he possibly say to her?

He was still wondering five minutes later as he sat at a plastic table staring at his uneaten food and heard a commotion behind him. Looking out the clear plastic tent flap, he watched a half-dozen men pour out of the security tent and jog toward the ATVs. Engines roared to life, drowning out the shouts of the operations guys diagramming search sectors on a large map taped to a whiteboard on wheels nearby.

Macy hobbled out of her quarters in a big hurry.

She had on a full environmental suit.

Clint shoved his tray aside, grabbed his mask and caught up to her just as she swung her leg over the last ATV. "What's going on? Have they found the monkey?"

"No." She fiddled with the ignition switch on the four-wheeler. He thought for a moment she wasn't going to tell him any more when she finally looked up.

Her face was pale. Her eyes looked bruised, tired. Her lips were flat, unsmiling. "A man stumbled out of the woods at one of the checkpoints on the logging road about three miles from here. He appears to be sick."

Clint flinched. His chest went hard.

Oh, God. It was starting.

"Scoot back," he said. When she didn't move, he waved her toward the end of the ATV seat. "Scoot back. I'm driving."

Macy tightened her hold on Clint's waist as the ATV bumped over a rut in the trail. His body was hard as a rock beneath her hands. Tension rolled off him in waves, crashed against her own.

"You don't have to do this," she shouted so he could hear her over the howl of the ATV as he pushed the engine past the redline.

"Like hell I don't."

"I can handle this."

"You don't even know what 'this' is yet."

He was right about that. But in the minutes since she'd heard, she'd imagined a thousand scenarios, each one more horrific than the next.

She squeezed her eyes shut, tried to shut out the pictures in her mind. "What if it's some poor hiker or camper that we missed when we cleared the forest? What if some innocent man has ARFIS?"

"Then it's one man, and we stopped him before he got to town and spread the virus to anyone else. It could be worse."

"Not for that man."

She opened her eyes. Clint was looking over his shoulder at her and for once, his expression was completely open, readable.

He was worried.

He pushed the four-wheeler faster. All she could do was hold on.

And pray.

They pulled in behind a mish-mash of vehicles that resembled a multicar pileup on the expressway. Except this was a two-rut logging trail of red mud, not an expressway. And there was only one casualty, as far as she knew.

Clint climbed off the ATV and headed straight for the

man in camouflage fatigues with yellow stripes on his shoulder. Macy tried to get a look at what was in front of the vehicles, but all she could see was a bunch of soldiers standing around staring at something.

She hurried to catch up to Clint, who had outdistanced her with his ground-eating strides.

"What have you got, Lieutenant?" he was asking when she arrived.

"Subject walked out of the woods twenty-five minutes ago, failed to respond to our challenges, failed to stop. He appeared incoherent. He was stumbling. There were visible signs of blood on his face and his hands. He was ordered to stop again, at which time he turned and came right at my men. They had no choice but to take him down."

"They shot him?" Macy asked, her voice high and tight.

The lieutenant scrutinized her. "They tranquilized him, ma'am. Used the dart gun we were given in case we saw the monkey."

"What will animal tranquilizer do to a human?" Clint asked.

"Depends what's wrong with him." She looked from Clint to the other man and back. "If he's got ARFIS, it's not going to matter one way or the other. Has he moved since he was darted?"

"No ma'am."

"He didn't say anything before he went down?" Clint asked.

"Negative."

Macy took a plastic box with a bright red cross on

the top from Susan, who'd arrived on another ATV, and started forward. "Let's see what we've got."

As she walked away, she saw her lab assistant give Clint a hard look. She'd have to talk to Susan about that. Macy was a big girl. She didn't need anyone looking out for her.

But right now, she had other things on her mind.

"Pull your men back, Lieutenant," she asked and he barked out an order.

The pack of bodies opened up, and there in the center of a circle of soldiers with rifles pointed down at him, face down in the red, rutted road, lay the man she had been engaged to marry until just a few days ago.

David Brinker.

"David," Susan breathed next to Clint.

Clint stared at the crumpled form on the pavement. All he could see from here was a cap of straight brown hair and a pale complexion, a pair of broken wire-rimmed glasses askew on the man's nose and fine-boned hands. "That's Brinker? You're sure?"

Susan nodded.

He took a step forward. Macy must have seen him out of the corner of her eye, because she held out a hand. "Stay back."

Every atom in his body wanted to go to her. She shouldn't have to do this. Especially not alone. But he did as she asked, not wanting to distract her.

In full protective gear, she knelt by the man in the road. Brinker, though Clint hated to think the name. Hated to imagine the man laughing with Macy over some private joke. Touching her casually. Loving her.

Betraying her.

"Be careful," he found himself yelling hoarsely. "He could wake up."

If he came to confused, pulled at her mask, ripped her glove...

Clint's hand automatically went to the Glock in his pocket. Could he use it on a sick, defenseless man?

He forced his hand away.

Hell, it didn't matter. He couldn't hit anything, anyway. He sure wouldn't risk hitting Macy. She was on her own out there, whether he liked it or not.

She had opened her medical kit and picked up the man's hand, was fixing something to his fingers.

"What's she doing?"

Susan whispered as if she were watching a surgeon in an operating theater. "She can't feel his pulse through her gloves, or use a stethoscope with the environmental suit, so she's putting a heart monitor on his finger."

Which at least meant he was alive as far as she could tell.

Once the monitor was in place, she watched the device in the medical kit that displayed its results, then began running her hands slowly over Brinker's arms, his shoulders, his legs. She turned him slowly, steadying his head, and pressed on his abdomen, then looked up.

"Susan, get me a backboard and cervical collar. We're going to need an ambulance—a ground vehicle, not a helicopter. I don't want to drop a trail of virus over Texas in an open-door aircraft. Clint, find me the closest hospital with a level-four isolation ward."

Everyone moved at once except Macy, who never left Brinker's side. It took nearly an hour to get a specially-equipped ambulance in and get him loaded up. By then he was shifting restlessly and moaning.

Clint watched Curtis and Christian, in their full environmental suits, load him into the back of the ambulance and Macy climb in after him. He stepped up just before the door closed.

She jerked her chin up and shot him a look that brooked no argument. "No, Clint. You can't come in here."

"Has he got it? Is it ARFIS?"

She sat wearily on the bench seat next to David's gurney. "I don't know. Make a list of the soldiers who were near him. Make sure they're quarantined, whether they were wearing protective gear or not. You scrub down good, too. Just in case." She looked left and right as if afraid of who might be watching, and pulled a plastic bag out of her pocket. Inside the bag was a pistol.

It looked to be about the same caliber as the one that had killed the pilot.

"I'll need you to take care of this, too. I found it in his pocket. Make sure no one handles it without decontaminating it first."

He took the bag, but his eyes never left hers. "Macy—"

"I can't think about it right now, Clint. Just do what you have to do."

Then she pulled the doors shut. As the ambulance pulled away, she flattened her gloved palm against the back window as if trying to reach through it, back to him.

Or ordering him to stay back. Stay away.

He couldn't guess which.

Chapter 11

"I know some people will go to extremes to get a few extra days off, but this has got to take the cake."

Clint recognized his partner's voice, turned to see Ranger Del Cooper's broad shoulders propped casually against the wall of the Houston Community Hospital intensive care waiting room. Del's fingers were stuck in the back pockets of his jeans, and one corner of his mouth was crooked up in a half smile.

"Well maybe if I liked the people I worked with better, I'd have been in more of a hurry to come back from leave."

Del chuckled, shook Clint's hand and then pulled him in close and clapped him on the back a couple of times when Clint reached him. "It's good to see you, too, partner. Look who else the armadillo drug in."

They separated, and Kat Solomon, the newest member of Ranger Company G, stepped up to give him a hug. When she let go of him, the Captain, "Bull" Matheson shook his hand.

"Any word yet?" Clint asked. He'd been in the hospital decon unit for the last half hour. He swore he wasn't going to have any skin left by the time this was over if he kept getting scrubbed down like that.

Bull shook his head. "I guess it's slow going, trying to treat an injured man without touching him."

Kat steered Clint toward a chair in the empty waiting room. "You look beat."

He felt beat. But things were looking up now that his teammates were here. He'd missed them.

He looked at her and Del, thinking this was the last time he'd be working with them as a team, and hating the idea. "You've been briefed on everything?"

Del nodded. "Brinker makes five of the six passengers accounted for. One still missing."

"Two missing. There's still a monkey on the loose out there somewhere."

Bull brought coffee for everyone. Clint filled them in on what little he'd learned since he'd last talked to the captain.

Bull sipped his drink thoughtfully. "Tell me more about this Dr. Attois."

"What do you want to know?" Clint leaned back and crossed his ankle over his knee, trying to look casual. He wondered if he'd pulled it off. His teammates knew him better than most.

"Is she hot?" Del asked.

"Hey," Kat admonished. "You're a newlywed. You aren't even supposed to think about things like that."

"Honey, I'm a male. Things like that are the only things I think about most of the time. Besides, Elisa says it's fine to look. I'd just better not touch if I want to keep all my fingers."

Kat smiled sweetly, which meant whatever she was thinking was pure evil. "If I was her, I'd be threatening a few other body parts."

"She doesn't have to threaten. She's all the woman I need or want."

Bull raised his hand for quiet. "Can we get back to business here, people?"

Too bad. Clint liked watching the silly grin Del got on his face whenever he talked about his new wife or their baby-on-the-way. He didn't mind a little of the focus being taken off him and his relationship with Macy, either.

As if thinking about her had somehow conjured her, he looked up to see her standing in the doorway. She was wearing surgical scrubs. Her hair was wet and her skin had that recently decontaminated glow he'd come to know all too well.

"It's not ARFIS," she announced without preamble. "His injuries are consistent with a major trauma like a plane crash, and the dehydration and confused state he was found in are in line with spending nearly forty-eight hours dazed and lost in the woods."

Clint hardly heard what she said about David's condition. He was more worried about her.

She was standing on one leg, balancing just the toe

of her sore foot on the ground to keep the weight off it. Her arms were crossed over her chest, but not in a defensive gesture. More one of protection.

Their gazes met for a moment. Held, then slipped away.

"Is he conscious?" Bull asked.

"Barely."

"We need to ask him some questions."

"It'll have to wait."

The captain sighed, obviously not happy with that answer. "Time is critical here."

She hesitated, gave in. "You can try, but I don't think you'll get anything out of him that makes sense."

"It's worth a try."

She unfolded her arms, nodded down the hall. "This way."

The others trooped ahead of her. Clint hung back. "Is he going to make it?" he asked when they were out of earshot.

"I think so." Her breath shuddered as if a weight had been lifted from her chest. "Thanks for asking."

Macy hung back as the Ranger captain and Clint walked into the isolation observation area. The woman Ranger—Kat they'd called her—had chosen to wait outside. Double airtight doors stood between the Rangers and the patient room.

"You'll have to question him from here," Macy told them. "There's an intercom system between the two rooms."

"I thought he didn't have ARFIS."

"It never hurts to be cautious. We'll keep him in isolation for another twenty-four hours to make sure he isn't incubating the virus."

Clint turned to her. His cheeks were tight, hollow. His eyes gray matte. "You don't have to stay."

"Yes, I do."

"Dr. Brinker, can you hear me?" The captain was an imposing man, in Macy's estimation. An inch taller than Clint, and built much heavier—bone and muscle, not fat. But he didn't have the hard edge to him that Clint had. There was a hint of compassion in his voice when he spoke. "Is the intercom on?" he asked Macy.

She nodded.

He tried again. "Dr. Brinker? We need to ask you a few questions."

"Mmm. Sick," David finally mumbled, and thrashed his head. His face was as white as the pillowcase he lay on, his walnut hair mussed and matted. A heart monitor beeped and flashed next to his bed, and IV lines snaked from his arm to a hook over his head as if the vines of the Sabine National Forest had followed him here.

"I know you're sick. We need to find out what happened. What happened on the airplane. Doctor?"

"Airplane." David licked his cracked lips. "No. No, crashed. Crashing!"

Macy's chest ached at the fear in David's voice as he relived the moment. His neck arched, his head bowed back.

"It's all right," Captain Matheson told him. "It's over. You're safe now. Did something happen on board the airplane to make it crash?"

"Fight. They're fighting."

"Who was fighting, Dr. Brinker?"

"Michael. Michael, look out!"

"Who's fighting with Michael?"

"God, it wasn't supposed to happen like this!" David gasped like a drowning victim who'd just been resuscitated. His eyes snapped open wide, round with fear. His fists clenched in the sheets. For the first time, he seemed to realize he wasn't in the airplane. Wasn't crashing.

And perhaps...he realized what he'd just said.

Clint glanced over his shoulder at Macy. Worried about her? Or just a cop cataloguing her reaction for future interpretation?

"How was it supposed to happen, David?" the captain asked smoothly. Soothingly.

David's tortured gaze flicked over to the window. Could he see her? Did he know she was standing by, watching and doing nothing while the Rangers battered him with their questions? Tried to maneuver him into a confession?

Her nails dug into her palms as she watched.

"How was it supposed to happen?" the captain repeated. His voice was deeper this time. Harder. "Was Captain Cain supposed to land where you told him without putting up a fight?"

Michael was a decorated veteran, Macy remembered. He wouldn't have given up his plane without a fight.

"Did you or Ty Jeffries try to hijack the plane, Dr. Brinker?"

"Hijack? You— I can't—"

"Where did you order him to go? Where were you taking ARFIS? Who was waiting there to pick it up?"

David tried to sit up, then fell back. His feet kicked at the cover. The beeping of his heart monitor became faster, more insistent. Macy took a step forward, but Clint stopped her without even looking back, holding his arm out in front of her.

"Who were you going to sell the virus to?"

"Sell?" The chords stood out in David's neck. His Adam's apple bobbed reflexively. "No! ARFIS—"

The captain pressed on. "Who put up the money? Was it a foreign group or domestic terrorists?"

"Terrorists! No." David was panting. His breath rattled. "I didn't."

"Do you know what their target is?" The captain splayed one large palm on the glass window and leaned close. David must have been able to see him. He stared right at him. "How many people were you planning to help them kill, David?"

David surged off the bed. The covers slid down his hairless chest, revealing a palette of blue and green bruises, scrapes and lacerations caused, most likely, by stumbling through the thorny vines in the woods.

"Nooo!" he screamed. His face turned bright red. His IV lines ripped away from the wall as he flailed his arms. The monitor screeched.

"How many people, David?"

Macy pushed Clint aside and stepped forward. "Stop it!"

An isolation-unit nurse in full environmental gear

strode into the room through a side door. She silenced the wailing alarms and checked the monitor display, then turned toward Macy and shook her head.

Macy reached toward the wall and flicked the intercom switch to Off.

The captain glowered down at her. "We're not done here."

"Yes, you are."

"Dr. Attois, that man has information that could prevent a national disaster."

"He also just had major surgery to repair several ruptured organs and re-inflate a collapsed lung. If he goes into respiratory arrest, or tears a suture and bleeds out, you'll never get that information."

"Macy." Clint moved to his captain's side. "I know it seems harsh, but sometimes you have to pressure people to get them to talk. We know what we're doing."

"You don't know David!" She studiously avoided looking at Clint. "He won't tell you anything if you back him into a corner. He won't talk to a bunch of disembodied voices behind a window."

Captain Matheson gave her an appraising look. "You have another approach?"

Her knees trembled. Her palms had broken into a sweat. She couldn't believe what she was about to propose. Couldn't believe she was helping them, when David was so sick. So hurt. But she'd seen the same thing they'd seen in his fevered eyes.

He knew something.

She had to find out what it was before a lot of people died.

She unfolded her arms, forced her shoulders to relax and took a deep breath. "Let me go in there. I'll ask him what happened," she said. "He'll talk to me."

Macy sat heavily in the chair next to David's bed, careful not to snag her environmental suit on the corners.

She picked up his limp hand, cradled it between hers as if the comfort she could offer would make up for what she was about to do. She tried not to think about Clint, watching her from the observation room.

"David?"

"Macy?" His voice was weak. He turned his head toward her, and his blue eyes were heavy. He'd used up all his energy earlier.

"I'm here, David. Everything's going to be okay."

He grasped her weakly and she remembered how soft his hands would be if she could feel them through the gloves. Not calloused and abrasive like Clint's. David wasn't as hard a man as Clint. Wasn't as strong. But he wasn't a bad man, was he? She couldn't have cared for a bad man.

"What's happening?" he asked. "Where are we?"

Macy stroked the back of his hand. He'd already forgotten the Ranger's interrogation. She hoped.

"We're in a hospital. You were in a plane crash, remember?"

He groaned.

"Why did the plane crash, David? What went wrong?"

She was careful to word her questions without accusation.

"Everything. The whole plan went wrong."

She tried not to stiffen. "What plan?"

He closed his eyes, shook his head. "No."

"Tell me what plan, David." She raised one hand to brush her gloved knuckles over his cheek. "I need to know."

He swallowed hard. The pain in his eyes stabbed her like a knife. "It was all for you. I was going to make you proud."

Oh, God.

His eyelids fluttered. "Knew you weren't happy. Knew you were going to leave. I thought if I could do something, be somebody, something special, you would stay."

Tears ran unabated down her cheeks. She couldn't wipe them away through the face shield. And she was acutely aware that the men on the other side of the glass were listening to every word. "What did you do, David?"

"The monkey. The one on the plane. He's got *antibodies*."

Her heart skipped a beat. "He survived ARFIS?"

"He never even got sick. I injected him twice. He's immune."

"David, with antibodies to replicate, we might be able to develop a cure."

He nodded.

She shook her head, lost. "So what was this big plan?"

He pulled his hand away from hers, turned his head toward the far wall. "I wasn't going to give him to the CDC."

"Were you working with terrorists?" She didn't want to believe it, but she had to ask.

He jerked his head back toward her. "No."

"Then who were you going to give the monkey to?"

"I made some contacts at Anderson Research. The CDC wouldn't have given me anything but a pat on the back for creating an ARFIS cure, but the big pharmaceutical companies would have paid me millions. I'd have been rich. Won the Nobel, maybe."

"David…"

"I know. I know it was stupid." His face pinched. "I just wanted to show you. I just wanted you to love me."

She couldn't react to that. Didn't know how. She needed time to process it. Space.

A place where she couldn't feel Clint's laser eyes burning into her back.

"What happened on the plane, David? What went wrong?"

"Ty. He went nuts. Tried to make the pilot land in the middle of nowhere."

"Michael refused?"

"They fought. Michael tried to get the gun."

"Ty had a gun?"

David nodded. A tear leaked out of the corner of his eye. "He tried to shoot Michael, make Bob land us, but Mike charged him. The shot went wild, then the engine made a popping sound and there were sparks and we started bouncing around in the air."

He steadied himself with a deep breath. "We crashed, and it was chaos. It was dark except for a few little fires burning, and I could see Cory still strapped in his seat, only his seat was upside down. His neck was broken.

Then Ty came out of nowhere. He was hurt, but he stumbled through the wreck until he found the animal habitat. He smashed it, grabbed the monkey and ran. Michael yelled for me to stop Ty. We both took after him through the woods, but it was dark. I kept running into things and tripping. We couldn't keep up."

Macy frowned. "What did Ty want with the macaque?"

"He knew how much he was worth, I guess. He'd overheard me on the phone with the drug company. He said he wouldn't tell anyone if I brought him to America and set him up with a job."

Macy felt like a well gone dry. She was tapped out, emotionless. Maybe this was why Clint seemed so detached sometimes. So removed. He'd faced this kind of insanity too many times. She couldn't imagine the toll it would take on a person.

She wanted to quit. To run. To hide. But there was more, and she had to know it all.

"What happened to Michael? Do you know who shot him?"

"He wouldn't give up. Kept after Ty even after the sun came up. We had no idea where we were by then. No idea how to get back to the plane, or find our way out of the woods. So we just kept after Ty."

"You caught him?"

"Michael tried to take him down. But Ty got the jump on him. He—" David's face twisted. "He shot him in the head.

"I—I think I charged him. I tried to hit him. He dropped the gun and the monkey got away. He went after it."

"How did you get the gun?"

"I went after it. I saw Michael. Lying there. I was scared. I thought Ty might come back. I picked up the gun so I could protect myself."

"But Ty didn't come back."

David shook his head. "I never saw him or the monkey again. I tried to go for help, but I couldn't find my way our of the forest. It seemed like the woods went on forever."

Her heart heavy, Macy looked over her shoulder, careful to train her gaze only on the captain.

He nodded to let her know they'd gotten all they needed.

She stood. "You're going to be fine, David. The doctors here will take good care of you."

He held on to her hand, wouldn't let her go. "It was all for nothing, wasn't it, Macy? Wouldn't have mattered to you if I had developed a cure for ARFIS, been a millionaire."

Pressing her lips together, she squeezed his fingers. "Everything's going to be okay."

"No it's not. Everything's gone to hell and it's all my fault."

Without meaning to, she met Clint's crystal gaze through the glass, though she could read nothing in it.

"For what it's worth, I did love you, Macy," David said, his voice scratchy, dry from the effort.

Looking down at him, Macy tried to remember what

she'd once felt for the wasted man in the bed, but could only dredge up pity at the moment.

"It might not have been the kind of love you wanted or needed. But I did love you."

When she turned toward the window again, Clint was gone.

Chapter 12

Now that they were sure Ty Jeffries had, indeed, survived the plane crash, Captain Matheson, Kat and Del were on their way back to Hempaxe and the Sabine National Forest to step up the search for the missing man. They'd asked the governor for more military helicopters to search the woods. The FLEER heat-sensing devices the army would bring to the party could find a live man even in the deepest woods by the heat his body produced. They had also put out a BOLO—Be On the Look Out—to law-enforcement agencies in three states in case Jeffries had escaped the area.

Clint stayed behind to wait for Macy, figuring he would hitch a ride in the CDC chopper they were sending for her. While he waited for her to finish decontamination and debrief with the doctors who would continue David Brinker's care, he stood before a window in the dim doctor's lounge. He hadn't bothered to turn the lights on. Just stood looking out at the Houston skyline against the black night sky.

He hadn't so much as moved a finger in five minutes. It was a technique he'd learned at a very early age. The more he churned on the inside, the quieter he became on the outside.

His old man hadn't liked whiners or complainers. He hadn't put up with temper tantrums at all, and he'd had a mean backhand. As a kid, Clint's ability to bottle up his sorrow, his rage, his pain and fear tight inside him and just stand still had saved him many a black eye.

And worse.

As a man, his self-control had earned him the nickname "Cool-hand" Clint, the Ranger who could stare down a dozen armed gunmen without flinching.

So why did the thought of facing one diminutive doctor have his heart pounding and his palms clammy?

Maybe because she had more power to hurt him than his old man ever had. She touched places in him that fists couldn't reach.

As evidenced by the way his chest contracted at the sight of her reflection in the window before him.

"Clint?"

He turned slowly, as if waiting for the next blow.

"I thought you'd gone back with the others."

He jerked his head once to the left. "Not yet. How's

David?" He couldn't quite keep the venom out of his voice when he said the man's name.

"Better." She walked toward him in measured steps. Wary steps.

Smart girl.

"His vital signs are back to normal and he's less agitated."

It was inhumane to not be glad about that.

He didn't care.

In fact, there was a part of him—an ugly part—that wanted David Brinker to suffer. Partly for the dangerous position he'd put the people of southeast Texas in.

But mostly for the pain he'd seen on Macy's face when she'd been questioning him. She'd loved Brinker once—he had no doubt about that. Maybe it wasn't the kind of love she needed, the kind that would last a lifetime, see them through good times and bad, but she'd cared.

Maybe she still did.

Therein lay the source of his discomfort.

Macy was a nurturer. It was in her nature to heal. Brinker was wounded. Would she be drawn back to him despite what he'd done?

The thought had his fists clenching, his balance shifting to the balls of his feet as if preparing for a fight.

"What will happen to him?" she asked.

"Nothing as bad as what he deserves, the greedy bastard."

Her ankle was bothering her again. She limped around him, scraped a wooden chair back from a worn table littered with medical journals and a tabloid newspaper, and sat down heavily. "David was right about one thing. The CDC wouldn't have given him any of the credit—much less the money—for a cure for ARFIS."

"And that makes what he did all right?"

"No." She twined her fingers. "But he was always kind of starstruck. He envied the doctors with the big houses and fancy cars. He is just as smart, just as capable as them, and virology saves a lot more lives than breast implants, and yet the plastic surgeons had everything he wanted. I think he felt…like he'd made a mistake with his life, sometimes. And yet he loved what he did at the CDC. It *was* his life."

"You're working awfully hard to make excuses for him."

"Not excuse him." She curled the corner of the *National Enquirer.* "Just understand him."

"Take a piece of advice from someone who's busted more bad guys than you can count. Don't try to figure out why they do the things they do. It'll just drive you nuts."

"David isn't a bad guy. He just…wanted more out of life."

"So does the junkie who takes a Saturday-night special into a convenience store and kills the clerk for the forty-two dollars and change in the till."

She scraped her chair back and limped toward him. Moonlight paled her dark complexion to ivory. The scent of Ivory soap reached him a second before she did.

He leaned forward an inch, drawn to her like the tide to the shore. His body tightened until he ached with the need to reach out and touch her. Claim her.

He didn't want to talk about David anymore. Didn't want to talk at all.

"You don't get it, do you? It has no effect on you." She raised her gaze to his, her eyes searching. For what, he hadn't a clue. "The lure of money. The attraction of fame. Temptation."

She inched closer. He held his ground, his senses filled with the sight of her, the sound of her voice. His mouth watered with the memory of her sweet, musky taste.

"You've never wanted something just out of reach so badly that you thought about crossing the line to get it."

She was so close he could feel her breath on his chest. She tipped her head back to study him, her lips pursed, and laid her hand on his chest. His heart thundered beneath her fingertips.

"You're uncorruptible. Unseduceable, right?"

His chest locked. Unable to draw a breath, he splayed his big palm over her tiny hand and pulled it lower. "Wrong."

Her eyes widened, luminous in the dimly lit lounge, as she felt just how seduceable he was a moment before his mouth crashed down on hers. He didn't give her a chance to accept or reject. Just parted her lips and plundered. Took what he wanted.

His skin itched with the need to claim her, to brand her as his own.

She made a sound in the back of her throat, something between pleasure and pain, and he looped one arm around her waist, pulled her with him as he backed to the door, reached down with his free hand and twisted the lock. Then he spun her until she faced that door, braced herself with both palms against the wood.

One-handed he yanked the knot from the drawstring at her waist and sank his hand deep into her surgical scrubs. With the other hand he palmed her breast through her bra and the thin, cotton top.

She threw her head back, almost clunking him in the teeth.

"I'm no goddamn saint," he growled in her ear.

But he was a fool. This was a no-win proposition, and he knew it. She could never be his. He would never be what she needed. Her heart was too big, too pure, and she would want to give it all to the man in her life.

Clint didn't know how to let a woman love him.

But he damned sure knew how to make her feel so good she'd never love anyone else without thinking about him.

The door to the darkened doctor's lounge was cool beneath Macy's palms. The body pinning her to it was searing hot. Clint's assault obliterated all thought, all sense—except of him. His hard body pressed against her. His hands were on her breasts and between her legs. His breath, warm and ragged, was in her ear.

The arousal he raised in her erased all the reasons they shouldn't be doing this from her mind. It stole her will.

Or maybe she gave that away by choice.

Without free will, she wouldn't be responsible for whatever course her life took, would she? Wouldn't have to look back and feel guilty over the outcome of the decisions she'd made, the way she did now.

She'd thought nothing could have made her feel worse than believing she'd caused David's death. She'd been wrong. Knowing she'd driven him to ruin his life caused a pain so sharp and so deep she thought she might die from it.

She'd known what she felt for David wasn't the kind of love a man and woman built a future on. Yet she'd accepted his ring, worn it nearly eight months before admitting to herself—and finally to him—that he wasn't what she wanted. What she needed.

Her relationship with David had been safe, comfortable during a time when she'd been too raw from the betrayal of her first lover to risk anything else. She should have known David would sense her ambivalence toward him. She should have known the lengths he would go to in order to win her true love.

How could she not have known?

Now his life was over, and hers might as well be, too. She couldn't bear the consequences of her actions. Couldn't risk ruining more lives. Especially not Clint's. He was too…too much. He was everything she'd lacked with David: heat, excitement, passion. On the outside, the Ranger might appear infuriatingly cool and composed, but she'd seen past that stony shell to the man inside. A man as unpredictable as an electrical storm, as charged as a lightning bolt.

He was everything she'd once wanted—and the one thing she couldn't have. Not now. Not with David lying down the hall, hurt and in trouble because of her. She owed him more than that. She had a responsibility, and it sat in her heart like a lump of ice so cold that even Clint's fiery touch couldn't melt it.

He must have sensed her withdrawal. His left hand slid under her shirt, tweaked and rolled her nipple until she had to bite her lip to keep herself from arching her back, pushing her breast deeper into his warm, rough palm.

"Let it go," he growled in her ear. "Whatever you're thinking about, let it go."

His right hand stroked the curls over her mound. Two fingers eased back and forth in the channel between her slick folds.

She whimpered. "Clint—"

"Shhh. Nothing matters right now but this. Just feel. I'll make you feel good, I promise."

"Clint, please."

He spun her around with a suddenness that bordered on violence. Her back was against the door now, her heaving chest pinned to his. Shadows hid the coarse cut of his nose, the slash of his cheeks, but his eyes glittered like silver discs in the moonlight filtering into the room as he lowered his head, fused his mouth to hers, stifling her arguments.

His tongue plunged into her mouth, reminding her of the way he'd plunged into her body once before. The way she wanted him to plunge again.

Never breaking contact with her lips, he stooped and picked her up. Her legs hooked around his waist automatically, bringing her body against the hot, hard length of his erection. She moaned into his mouth, desperate for more of him, desperate to have him inside her and yet knowing she couldn't. She had to stop this while she still could.

If she still could.

He broke off the kiss long enough to set her on the leather couch beneath the window. She gulped for air, tried to calm her pounding pulse, gather her wits to explain to him that they couldn't. She couldn't.

But it was too late. She hadn't yet even managed to string a logical thought together, much less speak, when she realized the bottoms to her surgical scrubs lay in a puddle of blue cotton at her feet. Clint was spreading her knees, lowering his head.

She nearly bucked off the couch at the first touch of his tongue to her most intimate recesses.

One of his hands found hers, linked fingers with her, holding her to earth when gravity seemed to have abandoned her. When her body wanted to float away of its own accord. His other hand joined his lips in the sensual invasion of her body.

Yes.

No.

"Clint, this isn't—" His fingers probed deeply, finding a cluster of nerves she hadn't known existed. Her head thrashed from side to side. Her heels dug into his back. "We can't—"

His tongue swirled. He sucked on her gently and her power of speech abandoned her in midsentence. Her whole body quivered. Her hand that wasn't held captive by his skimmed across his temple, around the back of his head seeking purchase but finding none in his short hair. With every stroke of his hand, each intimate kiss, her hips undulated against him, begging him for more even while her mind begged him to stop. *Stop.*

"S-stop."

Using his shoulders, he nudged her thighs wider.

Need gusted through her, whipping and lashing at the limbs of her resistance, gathering force and intensity like a thundercloud ready to burst into a full-fledged storm at any second. She reached deep for her resolve, held tight to her determination against the onslaught.

"I said *stop.*" Hooking one arm over the back of the couch, she dragged herself away from Clint. When his hold on her tightened, she shoved at him with her feet. A sob tore out of her. "Please. Just...stop it!"

Looking as dazed as she felt, he rocked back on his heels. Even in the dim light, she could see his face was ruddy. His breath came in long, hard rasps. "What?"

Unable to look him in the eye, she reached for her pants, arranged her clothing. "I can't do this."

Just like that, he went from dazed to enraged. His big fingers snapped around her wrist, stilling her shaking hands before they could tied the drawstring at her waist. "Can't do what? Can't get off on a crummy leather couch in a doctor's lounge? Or can't make love with me now that *David* is back?"

His sneer was ugly. Accusing.

Deserved.

She flicked a glance up at him. It was enough to see that his expression had set like concrete. The inscrutable Ranger was back.

"Both," she told him honestly. "Either. You're hurting me." She looked down at the wrist he held.

As slowly as if his hand were mired in mud, he uncurled his fingers, let her go. Then he lurched to his feet, wheeled and headed for the door.

"Clint?"

"I have to get back to Hempaxe." The words were as tight as a bowstring. "We still have a monkey—and a terrorist—to catch."

He stopped at the door to flip the lock, lingered a moment without looking back. "You're staying here."

It wasn't a question.

If she'd fallen down a flight of stairs, her head and her heart wouldn't have tumbled one over the other in such rapid succession. She wanted to call him back. Explain, as if she had words to express what she was feeling. To hold him, let him hold her and finish what he'd started. To give back to him what he'd tried to give to her.

In the end, she simply said, "Yes," and he walked out the door before she could tell him that she had to stay to talk to David about the monkey. She had to find out more about its immunity, the cure for ARFIS the animal might provide.

Not that his leaving without waiting for her explanation mattered. She doubted he would have believed it.

She wasn't sure she believed it herself.

Freshly shaved and wearing the new clothes he'd picked up on his way out of Houston that morning, Clint walked into room 143 at the Lonesome Pines Motel, where the Rangers of Company G had set up shop. Too bad he hadn't been able to purchase a new mood as easily as he'd acquired the jeans, boots and Western shirt to replace the blue CDC jumpsuit he'd grown to hate. The best he could hope for was that somewhere along the two-hour drive through the Texas woods, he'd managed to shore up the veneer of his control enough that the others wouldn't see he wasn't himself.

Those hopes were dashed within seconds of walking into the room. Captain Matheson was on the phone, pacing as he talked. Kat Solomon, the junior Ranger on the team, frowned at the screen of a laptop computer.

His partner, Del, took one look at his face and saw trouble.

"Well, well. Look what the armadillo drug in," Del said, sauntering across the room with his hand outstretched. "It's about time you got back."

"I wasn't aware you were punching my time card for me."

Del held his hands out innocently. "Just wondering if you'd decided you like the company better down at the hospital."

Clint knew he was referring to Macy. He let it go. The last thing he wanted to do was talk about Macy to Del. "What company? I caught a couple of hours' sleep in Houston—alone—then had to hitch a ride out here with a state trooper. Took a while to find one coming this way." Clint shook his partner's hand, but let the questions in his eyes go unanswered for now, opting to skip the personal small talk and get straight to work. "So what's new? Bring me up to speed."

Del walked with him over to the table where Kat was

sitting. "Malaysian government e-mailed us the background info on Ty Jeffries. He's got quite a sheet—smuggling, black marketeering, fencing—but he's never the main man. Always a middle guy, and the man who moved the goods. Never directly involved in whatever was going down."

"Does he have any terrorist ties?"

"None documented. Seems he's more interested in profit than idealism."

Clint scraped a chair back from the table and sat heavily. His heart wasn't in the conversation, but he tried to keep his mind focused. "So what was a man like that doing working for the CDC?"

Kat lifted her eyebrows in a speculative expression. "The ARFIS epidemic is a huge crisis over there. Lots of medical relief and goods coming into the country. People desperate enough to pay whatever it takes to get them, legally or otherwise. Seems like there'd be money to be made by someone who didn't mind exploiting a little human misery."

"If the local law knew about him, why didn't they alert the CDC?"

Kat turned the computer screen so that he could see the official file, with CI stamped in big, red letters beneath Ty Jeffries's picture.

Clint swore. "That lowlife was a confidential informant?"

Del grunted. "A good one, according to their local chief. Gave them some quality tips."

"For which they paid him handsomely, I'm sure. If he couldn't make money off the bad guys, Jeffries just switched to the other team. Either way, he wins. Pretty sweet deal."

Kat rose, stretched. Captain Matheson watched her stroll across the room and pick up her purse. It seemed to Clint that Bull watched his new recruit a lot, but it wasn't his business, so he stayed out of it.

"I'm going to get something to drink from the machine. Anyone want anything?"

Del and Clint shook their heads no. She started to walk out, and Bull covered his phone with one hand.

"Wait," he said.

She turned, smiled pleasantly, but there was no denying the bite in her words. "Did I forget to say 'mother may I?'"

Bull started to say something, stopped himself, then pulled out his wallet. "No. Get me a cola, would you?"

Kat took the bill he offered and left. Bull went back to his phone call, this time standing at the window, from where he could see the sidewalk.

The sidewalk that led to the vending machine, Clint presumed.

Del sat in Kat's vacant chair. "You look like hell."

"I've had a tough week."

"You've had a lot of tough weeks. Never rattled you before."

"Who says I'm rattled?"

"Maybe the fact that your shirt isn't buttoned right." Del leaned back, eyed Clint with an amused smile while he fixed his shirt. "So how come you hitched a ride here with a trooper? I thought you were flying back with the lady doctor."

Clint resisted the urge to squirm in his chair. "She had other plans."

"She stayed with the fiancé?"

"Ex-fiancé."

Del's smile fell. "If she doesn't have more sense than that, you don't need her, pal."

"She had her reasons." At least he hoped she did. And why the hell was he defending her, anyway? "But I don't need her either way."

Del studied him. Judging by his expression, Clint would say his partner didn't like what he saw. "Uh-huh."

Time to change the topic. "I didn't get a chance at the hospital to ask how Elisa is doing."

That brought Del's smile back. Nothing brought joy to his face like talking about his new wife. "Not happy about me being down here with the baby due in a month, but fine, otherwise. She's feeling really good. I've never known a woman to actually enjoy being pregnant the way she does. It blows me away."

Clint forced himself to return Del's grin. He was truly happy for his partner. But today, seeing Del so content made him realize how much was missing from his own life.

Before he could brood about it, Kat came back with the drinks and he shoved the thought away. What did he need with a woman? He had his work to fill the lonely days and nights of his life.

And if the question of what he'd have in a few days, when he lost that, too, drifted through his mind, he refused to acknowledge it.

* * *

Macy had been up all night and through the next day, talking to David whenever he awoke. Making notes. Skimming genetics Web sites on a borrowed computer. Her eyes ached. Her back ached.

Her heart ached.

For David, for the mess his life was in right now. What would happen to him when this was over? It depended on the outcome, she supposed.

And for Clint, for the way she'd left things between them. For the fact that the first time she'd seen true emotion in his eyes, it had been hurt. Pain that she had put there.

He didn't understand. How could he? She didn't understand herself.

She didn't love David. Not even a scrap of the old affection remained inside her.

But she couldn't abandon him, either. She felt at least partly responsible for all that had happened, and for that, she would see him through whatever the future brought him.

But as a friend, not a lover.

Maybe someday Clint would see that, accept it, but not now. Right now, even if he did understand, she couldn't be with him.

She'd left David because she'd wanted heat in her relationship with a man, but that didn't mean she was ready to jump into the fire. With David, she might have felt cold, isolated. But with Clint, she was deathly afraid she was going to get burned.

He was too intense. Too overwhelming. Overpowering.

"Ma'am, are you ready?"

The security guard who had been sent to drive her through the forest back to base camp on an ATV interrupted her ruminating. She nodded at him. She needed to get back and check on her team. It was dark now, but first thing in the morning she wanted to go through the debris from the plane wreck, see if she could find any of David's original notes on the macaque, study the data.

If she was lucky, work would keep her mind off her personal problems.

The guard keyed the radio microphone attached to the four-wheeler. "SG-four, leaving Checkpoint Delta for base with one passenger."

The radio squawked in return. "Received. Leaving Delta for base with one."

Trying not to wonder whether or not Clint would be in camp when she arrived, she climbed into the ATV and held on as she and her driver bumped and bounced over the rutted dirt trail.

They'd been traveling about ten minutes when the radio erupted with noise again, this time the voices sounding frantic. "Echo one, Echo one. We have target sighting. Repeat, we have target sighting in the tree line!"

Another disembodied voice asked, "Which target, Echo? Is it Jeffries?"

"No. It's the monkey. We're in pursuit. Repeat, we are in pursuit."

Macy's hand clenched on the roll bar. "Where is checkpoint Echo?" she asked her driver.

"About half mile east, ma'am."

"Take me there." She lurched to the side as he yanked the ATV around.

But it was already too late. She flinched with each firecracker pop that exploded over the radio, afraid she was hearing the death of the only living being that could stop the ARFIS epidemic.

"Step on it! And get on that radio. Tell them to hold their damned fire! I need that animal alive."

Chapter 13

Clint braced against the dashboard as Del skidded his four-wheel drive pickup to a stop in the mud at Checkpoint Echo. They'd been on their way to the CDC base camp near the wreckage to interview Macy's team, see what more they could learn about Ty Jeffries, when they'd heard the frantic radio calls from the Echo commander.

"What the hell?" Del breathed.

The place was deserted, the sawhorse barricades toppled into the dirt. Beams of light winked in the trees to the right. The sounds of shouts and people crashing through the underbrush disrupted the quiet of the forest.

"Over here! I think I saw him over here!"

"No! This way!"

Clint groaned heavily. "It's a freaking snipe hunt. With guns."

"Didn't they get word the monkey wasn't contagious?" Del asked incredulously.

By unspoken agreement, Clint and Del shoved open the doors to the pickup and made for the tree line, their weapons drawn. They pinned down the first camouflaged soldier wannabe they came to and barked out questions. "What agency are you with?"

"Texas State Guard, First Brigade, Second Platoon. Called up yesterday by the governor to help with security."

Great, Clint thought. Weekend warriors. The governor might as well have sent a troop of Boy Scouts to monitor the logging roads through the woods.

"Who's in charge?" Del asked.

"Corporal Terrence. He's over there." The man's head swiveled left. Then right. "Or maybe over there. I sorta lost track of which way he went. That monkey came at us and everybody broke ranks on account of it's got ARFIS and all. We woulda had him, if that lady doctor hadn't gone and knocked Jones's arm when he was fixin' to shoot."

Clint grabbed the man by the collar. Clint's pulse skipped a beat. "Doctor Attois? She's out here in this mess?"

"Don't know her name. Just know it's a lady doctor from the CDC," the soldier said.

Clint shoved the man away. "Get back to the checkpoint and stay there." He gave Del a furious look. "We've got to get her out of there."

Del laid a hand on his arm to slow him as he turned. "Easy, partner. We got a lot of trigger-happy desk jockeys running around in the dark playing at being soldiers. Wading into the middle of it isn't likely to do anything but get us dead."

Clint shook off Del's touch. "You got a better idea?"

Maybe the direct approach? Del turned toward the black depths of the woods and shouted, "This is Texas Ranger Sergeants Del Cooper and Clint Hayes. You are ordered to stand down. Do you hear me? Stand down! Return to your posts immediately."

"Who are you?" someone queried.

"Texas Rangers. Stand down and return to your posts," Clint repeated Del's orders in the same authoritarian voice his partner had used.

It seemed to be working. Most of the stomping through the woods had quieted. The yelling diminished. A couple of beefy young guys in combat gear, breathing hard, threw the Rangers sideways looks as they double-timed it by.

Clint squinted into the darkness under the trees, straining to make out a smaller figure amongst the shadows drifting out of the woods, back toward the road. He bit his tongue to keep from calling out, sure everyone in two counties would hear the worry in his voice that went beyond professional concern. Far beyond.

"All right," Del said, holstering his weapon and planting his hands on his hips. "Let's go help these guys to count heads. Make sure they didn't lose anyone out there."

Clint opened his mouth to argue that they couldn't

go back. That they should go deeper into the woods, look for Macy. But he couldn't think of a single logical argument for doing so, so he shut his trap before he stuck his foot in it. For all he knew, Macy was already back at the checkpoint.

Which only made him want to walk off into the woods even more, so he wouldn't have to face her.

Coward.

His old man would have laughed his ass off—right before he slapped him upside the head. Clint Hayes, afraid to face one little woman.

Clint Hayes, shaking in his boots because he was afraid some stray bullet meant for a monkey had found her in the dark. The image of her lying face down in the dead leaves somewhere had his chest heaving, his jaw locking.

With one last look over his shoulder, he turned to follow Del back the way they'd come.

Maybe she was back at the checkpoint, like Del said.

Clint hoped so. Besides being worried about her, he had a lot weighing on his mind. Things he needed to say to her, starting with an apology for practically attacking her in the doctor's lounge and ending with good-bye, have a nice life.

It wasn't like he had a claim on her. One night of sex in a fire tower, when they were both under extreme duress, didn't mean she belonged to him. She was a grown woman, free to be with whomever she wanted to be with. He could be adult about their relationship—or lack thereof. He could show her the respect she deserved. As long as it wasn't too late.

Please, let her be at the checkpoint.

He'd picked up his pace, in a hurry to find her, see for himself that he'd nearly had an anxiety attack for nothing, when another yell from the woods stopped him cold.

"There it is! Right there! I see it!"

Then Macy's voice. "Don't shoot! Don't shoot him!"

And the stampede started anew. Limbs snapped and leaves rustled. Heavy boots clumped along the clay ground.

Del turned back the soldiers from the checkpoint, ordered them to stay put, but there were others still in the woods behind them, yelling, running.

Del left his partner and ran toward the voices. Ahead he saw flashlight beams bouncing and blinking, cutting through the foliage.

"He's comin' your way, Tom."

"You flush him, I'll bag him," the second voice shouted.

"Flushing."

Morons. Did they think they were out hunting quail?

Clint sprinted ten more yards through the woods, tripping on roots and pushing vines out of his face. Thorns dug into his hands, his neck, but he ignored the pain.

"Macy," he bellowed, no longer caring what anyone heard in his voice. His cop instincts had kicked in. He could feel disaster creeping in like mist over a meadow on a fall morning. Silently. Stealthily.

His feet tangled in a bramble as he tried to climb a mound of thicket. On the other side, he could make out the silhouette of a soldier, his rifle raised to his shoulder, finger on the trigger.

"Lower that weapon!" he ordered.

Another voice, the flusher, hissed in a loud whisper, "He's coming your way."

Clint saw it then. The nervous little primate skittered along the trunk of a fallen tree, pausing to look back over its shoulder every foot or two.

The barrel of the rifle tracked his movement. The soldier's shoulders lifted, a sure sign he was about to fire.

"No!" Off to the left, Macy screamed. She ran toward the monkey.

Right in front of the soldier's rifle.

Clint yanked his foot free and leaped, hitting the man in the back just as a shot exploded out the muzzle. He saw the ground rushing up to meet him, felt the impact, but his gaze never left Macy.

She hit the ground with a soft thud. God, was she shot? He couldn't tell.

But she didn't stop when she landed. She rolled, lifting a weapon of her own, a handgun, and fired, but instead of a flash of fire and a bang Clint expected, her gun popped loudly and a dart ejected from the business end.

The tranquilizer hit the monkey square in the butt, dropping him in less than five seconds.

In less than three, Clint was at Macy's side, holding his breath as he turned her over, ran his hands over her legs, her arms, her body, checking for blood. Finding none.

She got up and brushed off her jeans, picked leaves

from the fuzz of her sweater. When he tried to grab her again, she spun away, marched toward the fallen monkey. "What is wrong with you?"

"Are you hit?"

She looked surprised, stopped for a second and appeared to do a quick inventory of herself. "No," she pronounced a long second later.

Clint's chest finally unclenched long enough for him to drag in some air. The oxygen that flooded his system was like gasoline poured on a fire. It ignited his temper. "What the hell did you think you were doing?"

"I was trying to keep those goons from killing the future cure for ARFIS before we have a chance to study it."

"You could've gotten yourself killed."

She knelt by the monkey, held his tiny arm between her thumb and forefinger, presumably checking for a pulse. "I didn't."

Clint's heart was pumping so hard it felt as if it might explode. She had no idea. She saw nothing wrong with what she'd done. Thought she was perfectly justified.

He reached down, pulled her up by her elbow. "Come with me."

"José," she argued as he dragged her away.

A few of the soldiers had found them. Clint pointed at one of them. "You. Stay with the monkey—I mean right with him. Do not let anyone touch him. Do not let anyone move him until the CDC team gets here with a cage. And for God's sake, do not let anyone shoot him, or your ass is mine. You hear me—" Clint leaned forward to read the man's nametag. "Cleburg?"

"Yes, sir."

He pulled Macy out of the woods without another word. On the road, he tapped Del on the shoulder then held out his right hand, Macy still caught in his left. "Keys," he said simply, and Del handed them over, frowning but silent.

Then Clint put Macy in the passenger seat, buckled her in and drove off with no idea whatsoever where he was going. Just knowing he needed to drive.

Macy folded her arms over her chest and stared belligerently out the front windshield. She had no idea where they were going and wasn't about to ask. She wouldn't give him the satisfaction.

Besides, from the look on his face, if she so much as opened her mouth, he was going to spontaneously combust.

They drove in silence for twenty minutes, maybe more, maybe less. It was hard to tell how much time had passed. Probably less than she thought, since every second in the tension-filled super cab felt like an hour, and she was determined not to lift her wrist to check her watch. She wouldn't give him that satisfaction, either.

Finally the truck jounced so hard on the two tire tracks she presumed to be some sort of road that she had to reach for the hand grip above the side door to keep from hitting her head on the roof.

His gaze flickered her way, just a quick glance, but enough for her to tell herself she hadn't lost their little war of resolve. He'd blinked, too.

A moment later, the walls of trees on either side of

the lane broke. Macy heard gravel beneath the tires of the truck and a pretty little cabin came into view on the shore of a glistening black lake.

Clint slammed the pickup into Park, turned off the engine and climbed out. The half moon lit him up like a statue as he walked toward the water.

Just out of curiosity, she checked the ignition. He'd taken the keys with him.

So much for a getaway.

As if she could have walked—or driven—away from him at that moment. The sight of him leaning against a rickety old pier rail, looking out over the water with an infinite field of stars shining overhead and little silver-crested waves slapping at the pilings underneath him mesmerized her. He looked so…desolate.

So alone.

She'd never been the kind of person who could turn away from a man in pain. That was why she became a doctor.

Somewhere along the way she'd forgotten that, she realized. Medicine had become about microscopes and single-celled anaerobic organisms instead of the living, breathing, multi-faceted, oh-so-complex species commonly called man.

She'd have to thank him for reminding her. One of these days.

Tonight, she'd settle for just being able to talk to him without causing him—or herself—more pain.

Slowly she climbed out of the truck and walked to him. "Your grandfather's cabin?" she asked after letting a silent moment pass at his side.

He nodded, still looking across the lake.

"It's nice."

He shrugged. "Haven't spent much time here the last few years. Kind of let it go."

"It looks like a sturdy enough place. Won't take much to fix it up again." A cool breeze flitted through the loose hair around her face. She rubbed her arms to ward off a chill. "Is there a particular reason we're here?"

He cut her a hard look. "I'm not going to jump you like last night, if that's what you're worried about."

Patting the tranquilizer gun in her pocket, she smiled and said, "I'm not worried. This time I'm armed."

She'd hoped he would laugh. Instead he only seemed to grow more sad.

"I had it all planned out. What I was going to say to you when I saw you again. How reasonable I was going to sound, how adult." He took a deep breath and tightened his fingers on the railing. "Then you stepped in front of that soldier's gun, and everything I'd planned flew right out of my head. All I wanted to do was scream."

"The world needs that monkey. He's the key to finding a cure for ARFIS before the disease sweeps through a dozen more countries."

He flexed his fingers, and some of the color returned to his knuckles, she noted. "In cop lingo it's called 'crossing the tube' when you move in front of the barrel of a gun like that. It's stupid, it's incompetent and it's a real quick way to get yourself dead. Who would cure ARFIS then? *David?*"

"Knowing what I know, you'd have done the same thing. I'm sure you would have. So this is really about David, isn't it?"

"You tell me. You're the one who couldn't drag herself away from his hospital bed."

"I stayed to question him! I needed to know more about his research and what tests he'd run on the monkey."

He started to say something, then cut himself off with a sharp jerk of his head. "It doesn't matter. You made your choice perfectly clear last night."

Her jaw went slack. "I didn't choose David over you."

Clint scowled and turned his head. She moved into his line of sight, where he couldn't avoid meeting her gaze.

"I chose *me!* I needed some distance. Some time to think." Oh, how could she explain the maelstrom of emotions that had her so caught up she'd been afraid she'd be ripped to pieces, and lose some part of herself forever. "I needed to get my head together, and I couldn't do that with you—"

Her cheeks heated at the memory of exactly what he'd been doing that had so distracted her. Macy saw the same memory swirl in his quicksilver eyes.

Knowing she was holding a lit match to a pile of dry tinder, she raised her hand and brushed her fingers across his cheek. "I stopped you because I'm afraid of you, Clint Hayes. When I'm with you, everything else fades into the background. No matter how important a thought might be, my mind can't hold on to it. There isn't a *me* anymore, there's only *us*. Only you, really. You fill up the room, the woods, the universe. I'm afraid one day I'll cease to exist altogether. Poof, and I'm gone."

He covered her hand with his, pulled the linked fingers away from his face and kissed her. Slowly. Gently. Chastely. Only their lips touched, and then only lightly. Then he lifted his mouth away and tipped his forehead to rest against hers, his breath ragged but slow. "There, you see? No poof. You're still here."

She smiled, and the smile welled into a giggle. "It's a start, I suppose." She lifted her head and fell serious. "I still need more time. A lot has happened in the last few days. I'm not ready to, how did you put it…cross the tube…again so soon."

He answered her with a nod. "S'okay. I'm a little gun-shy myself right now."

With their hands still linked, they strolled back down the pier to shore. Clint tugged her toward the pickup. "We'd better get back to camp before my partner sends a search party after his truck."

She lifted one eyebrow. "His truck?"

"He knows I can take care of myself." He patted the hood of the big diesel. "Baby Blue, here, is another matter."

"He calls this monster Baby Blue?"

"What can I say? The man is very paternal toward his vehicle." He opened the truck door, steadied her while she climbed inside.

"That's not really why we're leaving, is it?"

"No," he admitted, meeting her gaze evenly. She

waited for him to explain. "We're leaving because having you out here all alone, in my favorite spot in the whole world, on a warm, starry night is not conducive to me giving you time."

Then he closed the truck door and strode around to the other side, whistling "Yellow Rose of Texas" and jangling the keys in his hand.

Chapter 14

Clint should have felt more at ease now that he'd worked out a truce—or maybe it was more like a time-out—with Macy, but instead his stomach churned harder than ever. He never should have dragged her out to Grandpop's cabin. He should have left things alone. He'd been better off when he thought she'd rejected him cold. Now that they'd hashed things out, the door was open again to some kind of ongoing relationship.

The kind of relationship he never got involved in. Ever.

Sitting in a folding chair in Macy's tent, he slumped. She handed him a cup of coffee and their gazes brushed, sending a frisson of awareness clicking up his spine. Quickly he looked away.

His teammates sat in a circle in the middle of the

room, all of them watching him. Lord knew what they saw. With some effort, he screwed on an impassive expression. It wasn't such a big deal what they gleaned about him, but he didn't want to put Macy in an uncomfortable position.

She poured coffee for the last of them and then took her own chair for the powwow. "I was able to get a good bit of information about his work with the test subject, the macaque called José, from Dav—Dr. Brinker yesterday as his condition improved."

Bull leaned forward, dangling his cup in one hand between his knees. "You think that information is pertinent to this investigation?"

"Yes, I do."

"You mind if I tape-record this discussion, then?" He pulled a miniature cassette deck out of his shirt pocket and set it on the trunk in the center of their circle.

Macy shook her head. "No."

"So how come this monkey doesn't get sick?" Kat said.

Clint would have bet a week's pay that she'd been the kind of kid who did a cannonball right into the deep end of the swimming pool without so much as dipping a toe in to check the water first, except he could see from the looks on his teammates' faces that none of them would have taken the wager. The odds were stacked in his favor.

"Start from the beginning," Bull suggested. "None of us are doctors, so you'll have to explain as best you can in layman's terms."

She did, although the concepts were still complex.

Eventually, Clint lost track of the words, and just watched the play of emotion across her face. The way she pursed her lips to make an important point. The way her brows drew together when she tried to figure out how to say something another way. The way her chicory-coffee eyes rounded when she wanted to drive home a point to her audience.

At the moment, her eyes were very round.

"Whoa. Rewind," Del said, setting his empty coffee cup aside and making a twirling motion with one hand. "So you're telling us that the reason Brinker's monkey didn't get sick was because he'd been exposed to ARFIS sometime in the past and survived, and so he was immune?"

She nodded. "At least that's what David thought. When the monkey didn't show any symptoms, he said he tested José's titer, and it was off the scale."

"His what?"

"Titer. It's basically how we measure immunity. High titer equals lots of antibodies to fight off a virus. Low titer means you get sick and die. Thing is, the human victims' immune systems hadn't proven to be effective at all in fighting this particular virus. So when David saw José's titer he thought the monkey had some kind of superantibody that could beat ARFIS. He thought if he could get the antibody into a lab and study the way the antigen disrupted the life cycle of the virus, he might be able to recreate that action synthetically. Create a cure that would save thousands. Maybe millions."

"There's a problem with that logic?" Bull asked.

"Not the logic so much as the assumptions behind it." She leaned forward, propped her elbows on her knees and planted her gaze on the floor between her feet. "I ran some tissue samples on José last night. I didn't find a single bit of damage to any of his internal organs. Nothing. ARFIS is such a violent disease…there should have been some residual effects of his illness, even if he did make a miraculous recovery. I don't think that monkey's been sick a day in his life, and I certainly don't think some superantibody produced by his immune system beat ARFIS. The virus reproduces too quickly. In humans, symptoms appear within twenty-four hours. In forty-eight, death is imminent. In a simian, like José, the progression would happen even more quickly. There just isn't time for the body to produce antigen in sufficient quantities to fight the massive amount of virus."

Clint shook his head, trying to make sense of the medical mumbo jumbo. "So if José never contracted the disease, why is his titer so high?"

"That's exactly what I asked myself. And then I started thinking, maybe a person—or monkey—can't produce enough antibodies to kill ARFIS before it kills them. But if the antibodies were already there before the virus was introduced, the bug couldn't get a foothold, couldn't reproduce in large quantities, and the patient would survive."

"Is that possible?" Bull asked.

"We do it every day." Macy looked up and shrugged. Her brown eyes were round as copper pennies, making the hair stand up on Clint's forearms. Here came the bombshell. He'd bet on it.

"With vaccinations," she finished.

A tomb wouldn't have been more silent than that tent at that moment.

"How…?" Del finally began to ask, then trailed off, his forehead furrowed.

"Once we've isolated a virus, we can kill it and inject it into a live, but neutral, cell so that the body reacts to it, or just modify the live virus to make it harmless, and then introduce it to the body. Even though the patient can't get sick from the altered cells, the immune system recognizes the viral material as a threat and produces antibodies to fight it."

"I get how vaccinations work," Del said. "I meant how did that monkey get vaccinated?"

"There is no vaccine against ARFIS," Kat piped up in her usual ingenuous way. Her gaze jumped around the group seated in a circle like children at storybook hour. "Is there?"

Clint swore. "Brinker couldn't have seen this little inconsistency with his data?" He tried not to make the question sound like an accusation, but he was pretty sure it was obvious to all in the room that he didn't think much of Dr. David Brinker.

"I don't believe he had time," Macy explained. "We were so busy treating patients and trying to isolate the organism…. Plus he'd have needed to run tests that would have caused questions. He'd have had to explain what he was working on to me or one of the lab techs."

"Are you sure he didn't?" Del looked speculative. "We haven't really considered that one of the other members of Macy's team could have been involved."

"I've run backgrounds on them and interviewed them," Kat said. "Didn't turn up anything."

Bull kicked his chair back on two legs. "For now let's stick with Jeffries as our suspect. Doctor, you were speculating on how a monkey could have received a vaccination that doesn't exist."

"This is where it gets a little scary," Macy admitted in a low voice.

"Like talking about a bug that can kill you in forty-eight hours hasn't been?" Kat said.

Bull gave the junior Ranger a quelling look. "Go ahead, doctor. Explain."

"ARFIS only reared its ugly head, what? Ten or twelve weeks ago? To have a viable vaccine, someone would have to have been working with the bug much longer than that. Maybe years. I couldn't imagine how or why that could be. Usually scientists are more than ready to blab about their discoveries. Then I remembered what you said about terrorists."

"You think terrorists vaccinated the monkey?" Kat looked confused.

"To cut to the chase, yes."

Bull pinched his nose like he had a headache. "If terrorists were using this monkey, how did he end up in Brinker's lab."

"I've thought about that," Macy said. "And of course, this is pure speculation, but most labs have a policy that requires them to humanely destroy test animals once experimentation is finished."

"So…what? He escaped?"

"I don't think so. These animals are fairly expensive.

They're supposed to be destroyed, but I have heard of cases where unscrupulous labs, or the handlers that acquired and were supposed to terminate the monkeys, resold them."

Del cocked his jaw to the side. "Don't tell me. Ty Jeffries was the one who acquired David's monkeys."

She nodded.

"Okay," Bull said, his voice speculative. "So let's say the terrorists are experimenting with a vaccine or a cure. It works, and little Jose is immune. He's supposed to be destroyed, but instead someone resells him to Ty Jeffries."

Clint uncrossed his legs and leaned back in his chair. "Or maybe there was no middleman. Ty Jeffries acquired the monkeys for the terrorists, too. When he's done with them there, he sells them to David. Doubles his profit."

"Either way," Bull said. "Somehow the terrorists find out about it."

Kat's eyes brightened. "They go to Ty, want their monkey back. But David has latched on to this particular animal. Now Ty—and the terrorists—are sweating."

"So they threaten him. Come up with a plan to hijack the plane and get the proof of their existence back before anyone is the wiser," Bull finished. He shook his head. "Christ, where did they get an ARFIS vaccine to begin with?"

Macy looked at Bull and rubbed her arms as if she were cold. Or frightened. "That's the sixty-four thousand dollar question, isn't it? So I went over all the data we had so far on ARFIS."

Reaching behind her, she pulled a folder off the table and opened it, then held up two eight-by-ten printouts of what looked like inkblots to Clint, but which must have meant something significant to her. "ARFIS is a negative-strand RNA virus, specifically a filovirus."

She held out one picture to her rapt audience and set the other down behind her. "See the thin, snakelike shape and the looped tails? Those are common to all filoviruses, although the exact shapes vary. They also have lower-level details in common. At the chromosome level, they share genetic markers, just useless remnants of atomic structure that serve no purpose today, nevertheless that are always present. The thing is, ARFIS doesn't carry all of the genetic markers it should." She set the second picture down and looked at each of the Rangers seriously in turn.

"Of course, these results are preliminary. We have a lot more work to do and the facilities in Malaysia made it impossible to get complete data. We need a Level Four lab—the highest level of biohazard protection—to run the tests that will tell us for sure. But some of the genetic markers that a naturally occurring filovirus should carry are missing."

No one seemed to know what to make of that.

"Meaning?" Clint finally asked, afraid to hear the answer.

"Meaning that I don't think ARFIS is a naturally occurring virus. I think someone genetically engineered it."

By noon the next day, the CDC base camp was gone. Generators carted off, tents folded and packed, garbage

burned. The quarantined workers had been sent back to
their families with a strict warning about national security—as if that was going to do any good. By two
o'clock half the county would have heard tales about
their brush with ARFIS. Maybe half the state. A road
had been bulldozed in for removal of the larger pieces
of the wrecked jet. Clint thought he saw one of the security guards pocket a dial from the control panel, probably as a souvenir. The monkey, José, had been crated
and sent to a holding facility in Lufkin until he could
be shipped back to Atlanta.

On the slim chance that Ty Jeffries had succumbed
to injuries suffered in the plane crash out in the woods
somewhere, cadaver dogs from the state search and rescue task force had deployed that morning looking for
his remains, and state guardsmen were lined up in
shoulder-to-shoulder lines searching fallow fields and
farmland, hoping to stumble over a body.

They should all be so lucky.

No one was saying so, but everyone knew Ty was out
there somewhere in what searchers described as the
ROW—the rest of the world.

God knew where.

Bull, Clint and Del had been on the phone all morning with law-enforcement agencies from the Sabine
County Sheriff's Department to the CIA, with no leads
on Jeffries's whereabouts. He'd disappeared, and now
the Rangers were gearing up for a full-fledged manhunt.

Which meant it was time for Clint to let go of the silver circle and star that had been the center of his life
for the last few years, and his only goal during the re-

quired eleven years as a Texas State Trooper before that. He wasn't quarantined any longer. And this had become a case with global implications.

The world deserved the best on this job, and he wasn't the best any longer. To pretend he was fit for duty put everyone around him at risk.

But he didn't turn in his badge. Didn't say a word to his teammates about his inability to handle a gun.

He might have blamed it on foolish pride. He might have blamed the stubborn nature he'd inherited from his Grandpop and his father.

The truth was, he stayed because of Macy. As soon as he'd learned she wasn't going back to Atlanta with the rest of her CDC team, he'd known he couldn't walk away. She'd uncovered what might be the biggest terrorist plot since 9/11, and now she was working with authorities to figure out how to foil it. As far as he was concerned, that made her a terrorist target.

No way he was leaving her.

Standing on the tarmac at Lufkin Airfield, he watched her through reflective sunglasses as she said goodbye to her team. Even from a distance he could see the sorrow on her face, the moisture in her eyes as she hugged Susan and they whispered some girl talk in each others' ears, throwing furtive glances at him all the while, before they parted.

She would miss them, her team. Her friends. Seeing how open she was with people, how easily she connected with them, it was hard to imagine her locked in a sterile laboratory day after day. Hard to imagine that she routinely handled deadly pathogens in that laboratory.

She was tougher than she looked, he reminded himself. She'd handled herself in the forest. She'd handled herself in the hospital with her ex-fiancé. If things went south with this virus, she'd handle herself again.

He just hoped she didn't have to.

An attendant closed the hatch on the CDC jet and the plane rolled down the runway, gaining speed. Macy watched until it disappeared on the horizon, then came to Clint.

"I already miss them," she said. "I feel so alone without them."

He took her hand, walked her toward the parking area. "You're not alone."

They headed east on Highway 10 in a rented SUV, and in minutes, walls of trees appeared on both sides of the road.

"So what now?" she asked. "You want to know how to find a sneaky virus by fluorescing tissue samples, I'm your gal. But I'm afraid I don't have a clue where to start looking for a man who could be anywhere by now."

"Basic detective work." Clint spied a diner called Mama Joe's ahead and eased off the gas. "How do you feel about apple pie?"

"So-so. Why?"

He turned into the gravel parking lot under Mama Joe's blinking neon sign and cut the engine. "Because it's the one thing you count on to get a country waitress talking. And we need to talk to a lot of waitresses."

After an afternoon full of waitresses and apple pies, Macy was glad to settle into her room at the Lonesome

Pines that evening. When knuckles rapped on her door, she set down the glass of water she was drinking, tugged at the hem of her thigh-length nightshirt and turned the knob to see who it was.

All she saw was the big sole of a big boot plant itself on the wood with a *whump,* and the door burst open like it'd been hit with a ramrod. Her hand flew to her mouth. Ten years flew off her life.

Clint stepped over the threshold, frowning at her furiously.

"What the hell was that?" she managed to gasp.

"A demonstration of why you should always hook the safety chain when you answer your door. Especially when you're staying at a two-bit hotel in Nowhere, Texas, chasing terrorists."

Subtly, she reached for the water she'd put down, then jerked her hand up, sloshing the water in his face. While he was blinded, she hooked a foot behind his calf and shoved his chest, knocking him on his butt.

Wearing a smug grin, she turned around and walked to the bed, where she sat cross-legged on the faded paisley spread.

"What the hell was that?" he asked, picking himself up.

"A demonstration of why it's not good to mess with me after you've dragged me to every greasy spoon in southeast Texas." She lifted her chin. "I get irritable when I overeat."

"Hey, I didn't force you to eat at those last three places. I told you we could just get coffee."

"But did you taste that banana cream? Or the caramel apple? It was worth a little irritability."

"So says you," he said, still drying his face with his sleeve.

He turned around to close and lock the door. For the first time, she noticed the pillow and blanket he carried under his arm. "What are you doing here?"

"Moving in."

"So says you."

When he turned around, she could see he was through joking. "Look, I meant what I said about chasing terrorists. We don't have a real good handle on this thing yet. They could be in Afghanistan or in the room next door."

"Kat is in the room next door."

"Then you can bet Bull is in the room beyond that."

"What?"

He shook his head. "Never mind. I'd just feel better if I stuck close to you until this is over."

She started to argue out of habit and pride, but stopped herself. "To tell the truth, so would I. There's only one bed." Which sagged in the middle like an overloaded clothesline.

He looked down. "And a perfectly good floor."

"If you call two-tone green shag carpet perfect." The Lonesome Pines Motel—all twelve rooms of it—out on the highway between Hempaxe and Johnson City, Texas, looked as if it hadn't had its decor updated since it was built in the early sixties. Add to that, the rooms were about twelve feet square with painted cement block walls growing mold cultures in the corners and no padding she could detect beneath the carpet, and she wasn't going to let him sleep on the floor. She couldn't.

Sighing, she got up, pulled a pair of sweatpants out of her suitcase and yanked them on as if they were a chastity belt, then sat again and patted the pillow beside hers.

"Not a good idea," he said.

"You stay on your side, I'll stay on mine."

He climbed onto the bed as warily as a rabbit might poke its head out of its den with the scent of fox nearby. She snapped off the light and settled beneath the covers, trying not to think about the hard planes of the body lying next to her. Trying to ignore the slow spread of his body heat, the mingled scents of soap and leather and pine drifting from his side of the bed to hers.

Trying not to imagine how easy it would be to roll over into his arms. To let him hold the dreams of terrorists and snakelike viruses and corpses and trees, always the towering, dark trees overhead, at bay.

Macy had always been impulsive. Since childhood she'd been swayed by her emotions, led by her heart, not her head. She'd made a mistake with the man who had taken her virginity and her innocence in every other sense, the married visiting doctor. She'd made a mistake with David.

She didn't want to make another mistake. She'd told him she needed time, and she meant it. She knew it was the right thing to do, for both of them.

But that didn't make it any easier, and what her mind wouldn't allow when she was awake, her body took out of her hands while she slept. She woke to the feel of the sun streaming through the window and warming her back, crisp male chest hairs under her cheek and a hard male erection pressed against her abdomen.

She opened one eye to find herself curled against Clint like a kitten to its mama.

"Before you throw another glass of water at me," he droned. "I want you to know I am not responsible for this. You are clearly on my side of the bed."

She shifted back to get a better look at him, and found to her dismay that one of her legs was wedged securely between his denim-covered thighs and her arms were locked around his back. Under his shirt.

No wonder she'd slept so soundly.

"I'm sorry." She wrenched herself away, pulled the covers up to her chin even though she was still wearing her sweatpants and sleep shirt. Maybe that way he wouldn't see that her nipples were as hard as he was or smell the arousal on her.

"Yeah," he said, rolling out of bed on the opposite side. "I figured you would be."

She wished she hadn't heard the hint of wry disappointment behind the words. What had happened to her unreadable Ranger?

"I'm going to take a shower," he said in that same tone. "Don't worry, though. There'll be plenty of hot water left for you when I'm done."

What was she supposed to say? "I'm sorry" again wasn't going to cut it, so she let him go without saying anything and busied herself packing up her things. She didn't know if they'd be checking out today or not, but she figured she'd better be prepared. Besides, having something to occupy her mind kept her from dwelling on Clint.

In the shower.

Naked.

Wet.

Aching.

Stop it! She made herself smooth out the shirt she'd wrung in her hands like an old dishrag while she'd been imagining, pressing it with her hands against the bedspread. It was her last clean shirt, dang it, and now she was going to look like a wrinkled mess.

Maybe she was crazy, denying them both what they so clearly wanted, but she'd lost her confidence in herself, and in her ability to know what was right.

She straightened when the bathroom door creaked open and Clint strode out. He had yesterday's jeans on, but his feet were bare and his shirt was slung over his right shoulder. The play of lean muscles across his back mesmerized her. The narrow waist. The corded strength of his forearms as he filled a glass at the sink and swished water in his mouth. The—

Gradually she noticed something else. The water in the half-full glass he still held sloshed against the sides. His hand was shaking. A tremor moved visibly up his arm to his shoulder. A few drops of water splashed onto the counter in front of him.

Just then he glanced up and met her eyes in the mirror. Caught her watching him.

She cocked her head, confused. "Clint?"

"Jesus." The glass slipped out of his hand, shattered on the linoleum floor. He bent to scoop up the shards.

Her moment of shock passing, she hurried to help. He took a step back to pick up a large piece and she warned him. "Careful! Don't cut your feet."

"I can take care of my own goddamn feet!" He swiped at the glass fragment like a bear yanking a trout from a stream, then tossed it into the sink. Left-handed.

His cheeks were ruddy. His eyes hard, flat discs. She just stared at him, trying to figure out why he was so angry. In her hand, she held a piece of the broken glass. He grabbed it from her and threw it into the sink with the others, this time too hard. The piece broke into smaller fragments, several of which bounced back out onto the floor.

"Let me see your hand," she said.

"Forget it."

She ignored him, knowing she was risking his wrath, and reached for his hand, turned it over in hers, gently curling his fingers in and stretching them out. He stood stock still, and she wondered if it was of his own free will, or if there was simply too much glass on the floor for him to walk away.

"How long have you been having the spasms?"

His jaw went hard. "Long enough to know it isn't a temporary problem."

She probed his elbow, massaged his bicep, then moved his shirt away to get a look at his shoulder. He flinched, and it took only her a moment to realize why. She traced her fingers over the round, puckered scar just beneath his right clavicle. "This looks fresh."

"About six weeks."

"Nerve damage?"

He pulled his arm away from her and made one giant leap over the area scattered with broken glass to the safety of the carpeting beyond.

She followed him across the room. "What did your doctor say? Did he suggest a course of action?"

He snorted, pulling on his shirt with his back to her. "Sure. He told me start thinking about a new career."

The full weight of what he was saying sunk in, and sat in her belly like a lead ball. "You said you were on leave when you saw the plane crash," she said. "Medical leave?"

His silence was enough of an answer.

"You haven't told them yet, have you? Your teammates don't know."

"No." He whirled. "And they're not going to find out. Not yet."

"Clint," she said softly, an ache—for him—settling in deep in her bones. "It isn't going to get any easier with time."

"Funny, coming from the woman who keeps telling me how she needs time."

The quick change of subject stunned her. No, the truth of what he said stunned her. Fact was, she was holding a double standard.

He stepped up close to her, so that her nose was practically brushing his chest, and held her by the elbows. "You're not going to tell them."

Statement? Or question? She wasn't sure. She could hardly think with his heat seeping through her thin night clothes. His scent enveloping her once again.

His lips so close.

To avoid them, she stood on her toes and brushed her mouth across the abominable reminder of what a violent world they lived in at his shoulder. "Clint—"

A quick knock sounded, then the door swung open, banging when it hit the end of the security chain Clint had so carefully fastened last night. The crack was just wide enough for Del to stick his face through.

"Uh, sorry to interrupt, kids, but we got a lead on Ty Jeffries. We're on the road in ten."

Chapter 15

Del Cooper spoke over his shoulder so that Macy could hear as he pushed Baby Blue, his truck, over eighty down the two-lane county highway. "Kat and Bull hit the truck stop on I-10 early, hoping to catch the breakfast crowd. They scared up a long-haul trucker on his way back to Shreveport from Austin who said he picked up a guy matching Ty Jeffries's description two days ago and dropped him off at a farmhouse outside of Hope Springs. They've got the house under surveillance now. No sign of life yet, but they're waiting for backup to go inside."

"Who've we got coming?" Clint asked from the passenger seat.

"Who's not coming? We got local PD, county, FBI, you name it." Del took a curve and the truck lifted onto two wheels. Neither he nor Clint looked concerned, so Macy grabbed the door handle and gritted her teeth.

Fifteen hair-raising minutes later, Del skidded to a stop behind a dozen official vehicles parked haphazardly on the shoulder and in the center of the road. A uniformed deputy met them at the bumper. Clint and Del flashed their badges. "Captain Matheson?"

"Up there." The deputy pointed to a hilltop. "House is about a quarter mile farther down, around a curve. Good view from the hill."

They nodded and strode off. Macy ducked her head and followed, hoping no one would challenge her, but the deputy stepped in her path. "Ma'am?"

Clint reached back and pulled her around him. "She's with us."

The two men's legs were a lot longer than hers. She had to jog to keep up. By the time she reached the rise, she was out of breath.

Clint pushed her head down below the bush they were using as a blind. "Anything yet, Cap?"

"Still no movement." He checked his watch. "It's a farm, there are animals in the barnyard. Someone ought to be out and about."

"We going in?"

"Just waiting for Kat to call and tell me she's got the paper."

"Paper?" Macy looked from one man to the other.

"Search warrant," Clint explained. "We go in without one, anything we find will be thrown out in court."

She sat quiet and let them strategize after that. Not everything they said about tactical entry and booby trap sweeps made sense to her, but she understood enough to realize that getting a team into the farmhouse was a lot more complicated—and dangerous—than it looked.

The captain's cell phone rang. He answered it, listened for a moment, then said, "Excellent," and flipped the phone closed. "We're good to go," he told Clint and Del.

She wanted to blurt out that Clint wasn't good to go. The look on his face said he expected her to tell his friends he didn't belong on the mission, but she couldn't. He needed to decide that for himself.

She could only hope she didn't regret her choice to keep silent later. Like at his funeral.

When he had his gear on—about fifty pounds of Kevlar, an assault rifle and extra ammunition—he pulled her aside.

"Thanks," he said tersely, as if it hurt him to talk about it.

"Thank me by getting yourself out of there in one piece."

"I always do." He smiled, but she saw through it.

"We need to talk about this later," she said softly.

"We will." He pulled his helmet down. "Right now we have a plot to destroy the world to foil."

Plot foiling took a lot longer than she expected. She'd thought it would be like the movies. Lots of shouting, pounding feet. Maybe a battering ram on the door.

Instead, men crawled around the foundation of the old frame house on their bellies, inserting gadgets. Listening devices and cameras, a deputy told her. They wanted to know what they were walking into.

Minutes dragged into hours, and Macy began to sweat, though the autumn sun was weak and the sky overcast. Macy looked at the matching rocking chairs on the wide front porch and wondered who lived there. The chairs made her think it was a couple. Retired, maybe. Her stomach churned at the image of them sitting together with their gray hair, laugh lines around the eyes. She saw them holding hands, sipping lemonade and watching the sun set.

She shook her head to clear it. Man, her imagination was way too active. She had to stop thinking like that, thinking the worst. Yet still the images persisted in her mind.

Her stomach, however, had moved on, and begun to growl for its lunch by the time Clint walked back to her, his helmet in his hand. "The house is clear," he said. "But there's something you need to see."

She followed him until the county road turned into a gravel drive. He bent low then and quickened his pace. "Stay down and stay behind me."

"I thought the house was clear?"

"You're the one who's usually lecturing on precautions."

"Point made." She did as he said and wound up at the east wall of the house, beneath what appeared to be a bedroom window.

A man dressed similarly to Clint, but with FBI in big, block letters across his bullet-resistant vest, handed her a miniature monitor. A tiny ribbed tube led from the device to the window, where it was connected to a piece of plastic as flat as a credit card inserted beneath the sill.

"Use the buttons to angle the camera left or right, up and down," the agent explained. "Like a video game."

Clint leaned over her shoulder. "Pan left, to the bed. Stop. That's it."

When the image cleared up, she flinched as if she'd been hit. "Oh, God."

A man lay on the bed in the corner, his arms and legs flung wide. His shirt was plastered to his body as if he were soaking wet, and blood trickled from his nose and the corners of his mouth. The man was Ty Jeffries.

"Audio," the agent said, and tucked a bud in her ear. The man's breath sputtered and coughed like an old engine.

She'd heard that sound before. It was the sound of a man whose lungs were full of blood.

A man dying of ARFIS.

She put the monitor back in the agent's hand and tore the bud from her ear. "Get everyone back. Now. Call the CDC and tell them I need a Level Four team back out here, and have someone get me a bio suit. Fast."

"Make that two bio suits," Clint said, and his tone brooked no argument. "You're not going in there alone."

"Stay behind me," Clint ordered Macy, and prayed to God she'd obey. He hadn't realized how clumsy the full bio suits were. How the hell did she work like this every day? How did she handle lethal viruses as though she was plucking wildflowers? He would go insane. At least he didn't need a microscope to see the killers he dealt with. And he sure as hell didn't have to wear a spacesuit.

He needed to be looking for trip wires, checking for explosives, watching for motion sensors, feeling for pressure pads. The whole house could be one big booby trap. It wouldn't be the first time terrorists had sacrificed one of their own to kill a few infidels. But it was all he could do to keep from falling on his face in the clunky rubber boots sewn into pant legs that were too short for him.

He reached up to wipe his face, remembered he couldn't when his hand thunked the face shield.

"You okay?" Macy asked.

"Yeah." *Just getting a taste of what you deal with every day.*

Working meticulously, they made their way back to the bedroom where Macy confirmed the diagnosis. It took another hour to get Jeffries ready for transport to the same hospital in Houston that Brinker had been taken to, the only one in the area with adequate isolation facilities.

When it was over, a team waiting out front hosed off their bio suits, then they stepped behind hastily hung curtains, stripped and scrubbed their skin until it hurt.

Bull was waiting for them when they'd dressed and rejoined the troops. "I had ten men around that house. What's their risk of exposure?"

That was the Bull, concerned about his troops first.

"Low to non-existent," Macy said, and Bull's shoulders relaxed visibly. "The house was closed up tight and no one went inside. We'll keep an eye on everyone, but I don't think you have anything to worry about."

He nodded. "Did Jeffries say anything?"

"He was out of it." Clint rubbed absently at his shoulder. He saw Macy watching him and stopped.

Bull swore under his breath. "The monkey was clean and the virus on the plane was secure. How the hell did he get ARFIS?"

"Only one way to find out," Macy said, already walking back to the vehicles, shaking her head and fingering her long, wet hair. "Get him well enough to talk, and ask him."

"Ty, can you hear me?" Macy sat beside the bed David had occupied—had it only been two days ago?—in the isolation unit of Houston Community Hospital. David had been flown to a VA hospital in Virginia where he could recover under the watchful eye of the military, and Ty lay where he had been.

Outfitted in another full environmental suit, Macy held his hand as she had David's. On the other side of the bed, Clint, also in protective gear, watched with a wary eye. The Ranger captain, Kat and Del listened in from the other side of the observation window.

"Ty, it's Macy. Can you talk to me?"

They'd pumped fluids into him and given him stimulants to bring him around so the Rangers could question him. They were only going to get one shot. Soon he would have to be intubated to provide respiratory support, and he wouldn't be able to talk. After that…despite the fact that doctors are trained never to give up hope, Macy didn't think there would be an 'after that' for Ty Jeffries.

She squeezed his hand. "Ty, please. We need to talk to you."

He moaned. His eyelids flickered. His mouth moved, but no sound came out.

She dabbed blood from his lips, for once glad to have the double barrier of latex and rubber gloves to protect her.

"ARFIS," he mumbled.

"I know." Her chest tightened. It hurt her to see another human suffer, no matter what he was accused of. "Do you know how you got the virus, Ty? Where did it come from?"

"Bastards. Bastards!" His throat convulsed. "They gave it to me."

"Who?"

He mumbled again, and Macy couldn't make out what he said. With any luck the tape recorder running on the table would capture enough that they could figure it out later.

"Where did they get the virus, Ty?"

"Brought it with 'em."

"From where?"

His eyes were open now, wide and bloodshot. "Everywhere. They got people everywhere."

"Ask him what the name of their organization is," Clint said in a low voice.

"Ty, does their organization have a name? Who are they?"

"Secret. Secret. Don't tell me anything. I just take orders. Deliver things. But I figured it out. Know what they're doing."

"ARFIS. Malaysia was a—" He fell into a coughing fit. "Malaysia was a test."

Macy's heart lurched into her throat. Her gaze locked on to Clint's. His was filled with rage.

"A—" She could hardly say it. "A test?"

"See how fast it spreads. Vaccinate some. Infect some. See who dies. Dress rehearsal, they called it."

Clint leaned over, rested a gloved hand on Jeffries's shoulder. "Dress rehearsal for what?"

"Main event." His fevered eyes shone brightly under the harsh hospital lights. "Big city."

"In the U.S.?"

"They were going to wait. But. Plane crash moved up their plans. Big city. New York. Maybe Los Angeles. Chicago. Dallas."

Macy gasped. "My God, we've got to stop them."

"Too late," Ty said. "They're already here. Already here. Told me they were giving me the vaccine. Injected me with the virus instead. Bastards. Bastards."

His hands clenched to fists and he beat at the mattress. Tears tinged pink with blood scrolled down his cheeks. "Killed me. Freaking killed me and lied about it."

"Do you know any of their names?" Clint asked, his tone urgent. He seemed to sense they weren't going to get much more time with Ty.

"No," Ty sobbed quietly. "No."

"What did they look like. How many were there?"

"Four. Two Middle Eastern. Two with accents I didn't recognize. Dark-skinned. Like South African, maybe.

"Where did they go? Do you know how to find them? Contact them?"

"No." Ty was fading fast. He struggled to draw a shallow breath. "Too late. Too late."

"Macy." Ty looked up at her, his eyes barely open. "Back door. Heard them say they left a back…" He stopped to wheeze. "Back door to the virus when they created it. A way to kill it. Find it, Macy. Help me, please." Another wheezing breath. "Please!"

"Ty, what were they driving? How were they dressed? Come on, give me something!" Clint demanded.

But Ty couldn't. His chest heaved, but no sound came out. No words. No raspy breath. No air. Macy waved Clint out of the room and picked up the intubation tray to insert an airway to the man's swollen lungs, knowing it would sustain his life a little longer, but in the end, it wouldn't help.

ARFIS would win.

Chapter 16

By that evening Ranger Company G headquarters officially moved into a hotel two blocks down LaGrange Avenue from Houston Community. Clint flicked the light on in room 306 and surveyed the antique reproduction furniture, the thirty-six-inch TV, demure seascape prints on the walls. "*Hmph*. Practically a palace compared to the Lonesome Pines."

"Look," Macy said, flopping down onto the bed closest to the door. "Two beds."

"Wonderful." Actually he'd rather wake up with her in his arms again. He could use something—some-one—to hold on to tonight, with the world spinning out of control. He suspected she could, too.

As if she'd read his mind, her smile fell and she

stared at him through eyes that seemed to grow warmer with each passing second. Womanly eyes.

"Do you think we'll find them in time?" she asked, her face soft.

He would have liked to ease her anxiety with false reassurance, but she deserved the truth. She'd earned it today. "We don't have a lot to go on."

"But the guys who have the virus have got to turn up sooner or later. I mean, every law-enforcement agency in the country is looking for them."

"Yeah." He laid his keys, gun and badge on the shiny walnut-veneer dresser. "Everybody's looking."

He didn't add that the phrase *needle in a haystack* had never been more apt. In this case, the haystack was about the size of the continental United States.

He watched her watching him in the vanity mirror. She eased off the bed and walked up behind him. He turned to stand face to face with her, and caught the scent of her soap.

"I was thinking," she said. "Maybe I've been taking a lot for granted the last few days."

"Like what?" His voice sounded hoarse to his own ears. His heart slowed to a heavy clip-clop beat.

"Time," she said, looking up at him through a heavy fringe of lashes. "I thought I wanted time to figure out what I wanted. Turns out we might not have all that much time left."

"No one knows how much time they have left."

"Which is why I'm thinking now that we should live every day as if it might be our last. Because it just might be."

With a tentative stroke, she brushed her fingertips over the line of his jaw, down to his pulse, which leaped to her touch. He captured her hand in his, held it to his chest.

"Let me be real clear on this." Because he would self-destruct if he started something between them and couldn't finish it tonight. "Are you saying you've changed your mind about us? About me?"

Her smile was both shy and inviting. "It's a woman's prerogative, isn't it?"

That was all the encouragement he needed. He pulled her into his arms, luxuriating a moment in the slide of her hips, her breasts, against him, and then kissed her, pouring the gamut of emotions they'd experienced today—fear, frustration, disbelief, and yes, love, into each nibble. Each gentle caress.

He lifted her and carried her to the bed, laid her down and then reared back to turn the lights down low and peel off his shirt.

"I'm scared, Clint." The taut skin over her cheeks shone, luminescent in the dim light.

"Don't be," he told her, covering the length of her body with his. "Not tonight. Not with me."

Tears stung Macy's eyes as she pulled Clint closer to her, burrowed into him as if she could slip inside his skin. She needed this tonight. Needed him. Not just because she was scared, but because she'd finally realized what she should have seen a long time ago: she was better with him. She felt more alive than she ever had.

Maybe it was adrenaline released into her system because of everything that had happened, was happening.

Maybe it was fear driving her into the arms of someone bigger, stronger, who could protect her from shadowy terrorists. But she didn't think so.

What she felt for Clint felt real. True to her heart.

Now that she realized that, she regretted every second she'd spent apart from him. Every time she'd pushed him away. She wouldn't make that mistake again. Not with ARFIS out there in the hands of terrorists. Who knew which day, which minute, which embrace would be their last?

"Make love to me, Clint?" she asked.

He lowered his head to the crook of her neck and teased the sensitive skin there. "All night long, darlin'. All night long."

He made good on his promise, first undressing her one piece of clothing at a time and worshipping the body he bared. He kissed her breasts, the backs of her knees, her feet. He kindled fire in her blood, skimming his hands from her ribcage, across the dip at her waist, over her hips. He suckled her breasts, tugging on the tight cord of desire that ran from her nipples to her womb. And when he finally parted her thighs and plunged into her, he gave her everything she'd ever wanted in a man—honor, compassion, courage and love.

She felt his love in every lunge, every rock of his hips against hers, every word of passion whispered in her ear.

And she felt his heat. Flames licked at her heels. His hands left scorching trails over her breasts, down her abdomen past her navel to the sensitive spot just above where he penetrated her. Her body burned with his, but this time she wasn't afraid. He moved his thumb and forefinger in small circles, and she stepped over, let herself go, falling gladly into the fire.

With the inferno blazing around her and inside her, she struggled to hang on to conscious thought. She wanted to give back as much as he gave her, show him the same love, twofold, so she lifted her head and murmured encouragement. She clasped him while spasms shook her and her breath roared in her ears. She heightened his sensation by sliding her hands as far down his back as she could reach and pulling him close, drawing on his hard, male nipples with her supple lips.

"Take what you need, Clint," she told him with what was left of her breath. "Take what you need."

As her release faded, his hit hard. He groaned and shuddered. His back went stiff and he buried himself one last time inside her, impossibly deep, impossibly hard. She held him there, stroking the back of his neck and murmuring soothing words, wishing she would never have to let him go.

But all too soon he levered his weight off her and rolled to the side. In an instant, she missed the contact. She felt as though part of herself was missing, and she reached for him, mewling a needy sound.

He pulled her on top of him and smiled. "You didn't think we were done, did you?"

She toyed with him idly, knowing it was too soon to get much result, but enjoying the pleasure written on his face as clearly as a grade-school teacher's ABC.

He pulled her down to his chest and kissed the shells of her ears, her eyelids.

My, how she loved this man. She just hoped she had time to show him how much. Preferably many years.

But if that wasn't to be, she planned to make the most of the few hours she had.

"Not by a long shot did I think we were done," she said, and increased the pressure and pace of her stroking. "You promised me all night long, and I plan to hold you to your word."

Macy and Clint rose quietly in the morning. They made love against the shower wall without words, the hot water streaming over their bodies, into their eyes, blinding them to everything except sensation. The feel of their bodies joining, slapping together in a perfect rhythm. A perfect union. It was a morning Macy would never forget. One of those idyllic moments in life where all a person's problems disappear, no matter how grave.

Like spending the moment in a snow globe, she thought with a small smile. Where everything was beautiful and clean.

At least for a little while.

They picked up coffee and bagels on the hotel's continental breakfast table and took them to the hospital, where they were supposed to meet the rest of the team at eight. Bull was pacing, his cell phone to his ear when they walked into the old treatment room the ICU staff had cleared for the Rangers to use. Kat and Del sat at desks, hunched over laptop computers.

"Any news?" Clint asked his partner.

"Not much. Kat is checking with customs to see what foreign nationals—especially Middle Eastern and

African—have come into Texas through the Houston and Dallas airports in the last five days, but I don't expect to get a hit there. We don't know how long these guys have been in the country, and they could have made their entry in some other city, and then taken a domestic flight here."

"So Del is checking rental-car agencies," Kat said brightly. "Trying to find out if anyone rented a car with a foreign driver's license."

"What about the farmhouse? Did the cleanup team find anything?"

Del hesitated, then said, "Nothing that would tell us who they are or where they went." He glanced at Clint, then at Macy. She had the feeling some unspoken communication had just occurred between them. Cop communication.

"What?" she asked.

"She may as well hear it all," Clint said. "She's in this as deep as us."

Del nodded once. "The bodies of the homeowners were in the basement."

Macy sucked in a breath. "My God. ARFIS?"

"No. They'd been shot with small-caliber weapons."

Macy felt like someone had stuck a fist in her diaphragm. The rocking chairs. She knew she should feel sad about the deaths of two innocent people, but for some reason what stood out in her mind was the incomprehensible loneliness of the image of those two rocking chairs on the porch that would now sit forever empty, only the wind to rock them.

"It looks like our bad guys picked the place at random. Somewhere out of the way, but that Jeffries could get to without too much trouble. His text pager was in the bedroom where we found him with that address on it. They must have contacted him, ordered him in." Del glanced back at his screen and tapped a few keys. "We've got BOLOs out on our unknown subjects, but without more of a description than two Middle Easterners and two Africans, there isn't going to be much anyone can do. We don't even know if the four of them are still together. They could have split up."

Clint grunted. "Taken the virus to two cities, or four. Nice thought, Del. Thanks for that."

"Aim to please," Del said, his lips set in a grim line.

Captain Matheson snapped his flip phone shut. "Dr. Attois, I need you to check on our patient. Talk to his doctors. See if there's any way we can get him to answer a few more questions. Anything we can give him to bring him around."

"I'll check," she promised, "but it's doubtful. He should be nearly comatose by now, and it won't be long before the seizures begin."

She didn't have to say that death would soon follow. Excusing herself, she left them to their detective work and went to suit up for the iso bay. Outside the door, she double- and triple-checked the seals around the tops of both pairs of the gloves she wore, a heavier pair not unlike dishwashing gloves on top and a thinner latex set next to her skin, then fortified herself with a deep breath against the despair she was sure to encounter inside and pushed the button to unseal the airlock.

A nurse in full gear stood by Ty's bedside administering a blood coagulant. When she was done, Macy asked. "Could I see his chart, please?"

The woman set down the used hypodermic and handed her the clipboard with a pen attached on a string, then excused herself from the room.

A glance at the patient record told Macy that Ty's condition was as bad as she'd expected. His fever had been over 104 degrees for nearly ten hours, and was climbing steadily. His pulse was too fast, his blood pressure too low.

She lifted one of his eyelids. The fine blood vessels of the sclera had ruptured, turning the whites of his eyes deep red and brown like a monster in a picture show. Only this man was only a monster by his deeds, not his genetics. It disturbed Macy to see the human body so abused. To see a human being suffering.

To her surprise, his other eye fluttered open. He choked on the tube in his throat. Trying to speak?

"Ty? Can you hear me?" He gagged again. "You can't talk because we have a tube in your throat to keep your airway open. If you can hear me, if you understand, move your right hand."

The fingers on his right hand wiggled.

Behind her in the observation room, Clint stepped to the window and laid his palm against the glass.

Encouragement? Or a warning?

No time to find out. Ty's lucidity wouldn't last long. She was amazed he was coherent at all at this stage of the disease's progression, but elated nonetheless. She'd take every second she could get to try to pull information from him. Millions of lives were at stake.

"Who did this to you, Ty?" She leaned over him, but realized he couldn't see her. The pressure in his eyes had blinded him. His hand moved, but she didn't have any way to interpret the meaning of his gestures. She realized she'd have to simplify the questions to get any meaningful information out of him. "Did they just come into the country, or have they been here a long time? Move your hand if they've been here a long time."

His fingers quit twitching.

"Good. They came into the country recently." She searched her mind for anything else that might help the Rangers prevent a biological attack in the U.S. "Do you know how they're going to release the virus? Move your hand if it's in the air, stay still if they're planning to contaminate the water."

Again, his fingers were still.

"Water." She threw a frightened look at Clint. "My God, they're going after the water." She didn't know why that shocked her so much. Seeding ARFIS into the water was no worse than releasing it into the air in a populated area. She guessed knowing the plan of attack just made the possibility seem all that more real.

Ty squirmed, becoming agitated. She needed to hurry. Get more information before he drifted away from her. But what else could she ask?

"When?" the next question popped into her mind and out of her mouth at the same instant. "Do you know when they're going to release the virus? Move your hand if it's more than a week away."

Oh, no. His fingers didn't move. She wanted his fingers to move. She willed his fingers to move. They needed more time. More than a week!

"What day, Ty? Move your fingers on the day." Today was Thursday, she thought. "Friday?" Nothing. "Saturday?" Nothing. "Sunday?"

His index finger tapped once on the blanket.

"Sunday." Her heart hammered so hard she thought it might burst right through her suit. Just three days.

Her breath hitched. A lump clogged her throat.

Ty's squirming became thrashing. His chest spasmed. His head bowed back and the chords of his neck stood out.

"Where?" She shouted at him, hoping he would hear her over his pain. "Move your hand if the target is east of the Mississippi."

Both his hands moved. They swung wildly, but she didn't think it meant anything. He was delirious, fighting demons she couldn't see. Fighting death.

"Please, Ty. Try to concentrate a minute longer. Don't let the men who did this to you get away with it. Don't let them kill thousands more! Move your hand if the target city is west of the Mississippi."

He made a strangled sound, full of animal rage. His eyes bulged, bloody and blind. He raised up—God knew where he found the strength—and flailed at the air as if he were being attacked by invisible birds. His IV stand clanged to the floor. Tubes tangled around his neck. His arm crashed against the table next to the bed, sending a tray sailing into the wall.

Macy knew she was in trouble when Ty got hold of her arm, just above the wrist. His grip was surprisingly strong, fueled by insanity and pain. She didn't dare wrench herself away by force for fear he would tear her suit. She clawed at his fingers, trying to pry them away. All the while she could feel Clint's gaze on her. She heard him, muffled through the glass.

"Macy!" His fists thumped on the window.

Ty's free hand continued to flap and wave. He hit the table again, this time closed his hand over something. At first Macy thought it was a pen—dangerous enough for someone whose life depends on not allowing so much as a microscopic puncture to her rubber suit, much less a gaping tear—then he swung his arm up, and she got a better look at what he held a second before it plunged toward the back of her hand.

The hypodermic the nurse had left behind. A needle which had, just minutes before, been inserted directly into the bloodstream of a man dying of the most lethal pathogen to surface on the face of the earth in fifty years.

Chapter 17

Christ. Oh, Christ.

Clint threw himself at the window between the observation area and Ty's room, but the half-inch Plexiglas barrier held. He watched in horror as Macy yanked her arm away from Jeffries, but not before it was too late. At least he thought it was too late.

Please, God, don't let him have punctured her glove.

He ran. Skidded around the corner and hit the button to open the airlock door that led into the decontamination area, but the door remained closed. A warning light blinked overhead: Occupied.

"Damn." Through the peephole, he could see her in the first chamber, still in her suit, her arms held out to the side as the Lysol shower sprayed her down. Then she hooked the hanger to the loop on the suit at the back of her neck, unzipped the bodice and stepped out, leaving the rubberized coveralls, attached boots and outer gloves and all to drip dry. The glove of the left hand bore an obvious tear.

She was already stripping off her inner layer of gloves, the latex pair, carrying one with her as she stepped behind the curtain where he knew she would strip out of her surgical scrubs and rinse her body the same way she'd rinsed the suit.

He braced his hands on the doorframe and hung his head. His heart ricocheted off the walls of his chest with startling ferocity.

A minute passed like an eon. Two. Then he heard the airlock door on the other side of the decontamination area click open and the warning light over his head winked off.

He caught up to her in the dressing room. She'd put on a clean pair of scrubs and stood at a sink pouring bleach on her hands directly from the bottle and rubbing it in.

"Did it puncture the inner glove? Break the skin?"

"I don't know." She looked over her shoulder at him. Her face was white as bone. She nodded toward the rumpled piece of latex on the counter. "Check the glove for holes. Pour some more bleach on it first."

He doused the latex while she scrubbed some more, then pinched the skin on the back of her hand. "No blood. I don't see a wound," she sounded calm.

"That's good. That's good, right?" He could hardly talk. Adrenaline had his chest heaving for air.

"Good, but not a guarantee. The bleach is stinging

me, as if it got in a wound. The needle may have pierced the epithelial layer, the skin, just not gone deep enough to hit a capillary and draw blood. The virus would still transfer."

"Dammit, what was a needle doing lying around in there, anyway?"

"I interrupted the nurse and she forgot it. It was—" Tight-lipped, she shook her head. "Just check the glove."

He opened the scrap of latex at the wrist and held it under a slow-running faucet, the way he'd seen Susan do once at the camp. When the glove was full, he held the end closed and squeezed it gently, watching closely to see if any water leaked out. If it leaked, there was a hole.

He forgot to breathe as he squeezed, and then the world tipped crazily beneath his feet as a tiny bead of water appeared on the surface of the glove and plopped into the sink below.

"Are you sure you're ready for this?"

Clint sat facing Macy in a plastic chair identical to the one she was seated in. He reached out and took her hands in his.

She swallowed and nodded, her head bowed. Her hair hung over her eyes like a curtain, shielding her from his probing gray gaze. He swept back the heavy mass and lifted her chin.

"You don't have to do it. I can tell them."

"I can do it," she dragged in a heavy breath and straightened up, more for his benefit than because she felt like it. "It's okay. It's part of the risk I accepted when I signed on at the CDC. I've always known this could happen."

"It's not okay. Not even close."

"Let's go. I'd like to get it over with."

"Macy, we need to talk about this."

A spurt of anger flashed through her. She lurched out of her chair. "I don't want to talk about it! I just want to— Want to…"

"Pretend it isn't happening? That it didn't happen? You can only put off facing the truth for so long. Believe me, I've had a lot of experience trying, lately."

Her gaze automatically landed on his shoulder, the spot where his shirt hid the scar from a bullet wound. She felt for him, knew that he felt crippled because he didn't have full control of his body. But he could hardly understand how she felt at this moment, facing the almost certainty of contracting a lethal disease.

"I don't think you can compare your situation and mine."

"I wouldn't begin to. If nothing else, the last few days have taught me that there are a lot more important things in life than having a steady gun hand."

He moved in close to her, eased her into his arms.

Some part of her told her to resist. If she didn't have the strength to let him go now, she never would. But she couldn't. He just felt too good. Too strong, and she needed strength right now. She needed all the strength she could get.

"I just don't want you to push me away," he said against her neck, rocking her. "I want to be there for you."

"You can't be there. No one can. I'm not contagious now, but in a few hours, the virus will have spread to my lungs. I'll have to be isolated."

His arms tightened. His voice hardened. "You're not going to do this alone. I'll suit up. I'll be there with you every minute."

The thought of him sitting beside her while she thrashed on the bed, wild-eyed and delirious like Ty Jeffries turned her stomach. Vanity? She didn't think so.

She didn't want him to have to watch her die the way they'd watched Ty Jeffries die just minutes ago through the observation window. She didn't want him to remember her that way.

"You have terrorists to catch, Clint. There are a lot more lives at stake than just mine."

Clint set her back from him and framed her face with his hands. "Yours is the only one I care about. Don't you get that?"

The admission brought a new stream of tears to her cheeks. Her steely-eyed Ranger, the man who never let on he had feelings, much less displayed them, was looking at her with such tough tenderness, such ferocious love, than the sight of him made her heart swell and ache.

"First thing you're going to do after we talk to the team is give the doctors here a crash course on this bug. You've got to teach them everything they need to know in order to treat you. You're the expert."

"There isn't much they can do other than standard supportive therapy."

His hands moved from her face to her shoulders. He

shook her lightly. "There must be something else. You weren't just sitting back and watching people suffer in Malaysia. I know you. What were you trying? What did you think might make a difference that you didn't have a chance to try before you left?"

She shuffled uneasily. "We tried the standard antiviral treatments. None of them showed any substantial results."

"Brinker thought he could create a cure using the monkey's antibodies. What about that?"

"He might have been able to create a cure. In eight or ten months. But not eight or ten hours. I'm not the only one who needs to face the truth, here, Clint. You're going to have to accept this, too."

His hands tightened on her shoulders. Myriad emotions played across his face in the span of a heartbeat—fear, anger…grief. Then he pulled her into a bear hug that felt like it could last all winter, except it was interrupted by a noise from the open doorway.

Del cleared his throat again. The captain and Kat stood behind him, open curiosity in their stares.

"You said you needed to talk to us," Del said to Clint.

Macy let go of Clint reluctantly and turned to his friends. She might be pretending there was nothing wrong to herself, but she wanted them to know the truth.

Clint was going to need them for the next forty-eight hours.

She pulled her shoulders back. "Actually *I* need to talk to you."

Clint linked his hand in hers in silent support. She squeezed gratefully.

"I wanted to let you know that I won't be able to help with the investigation the way I'd hoped." Her voice cracked on the last word. She bit her lip to steady herself and looked up at Clint for the strength to go on.

"I had a little accident in the iso room."

For twelve agonizing hours, all Clint could do was watch the clock and will the hands to move faster. Then when the incubation period was up, and Macy's blood test came back positive for ARFIS, all he wanted to do was turn them back.

It wasn't as if the results were a surprise. He should have been prepared. But how does one prepare for news like that?

Macy accepted the findings with a courage that both made him proud and tore his heart in two. He'd suited up and waited in an isolation unit with her as he'd promised, but eventually she'd wanted to know what was happening with the investigation, so he'd returned to his teammates to check.

And to get a little counseling.

Bull was on his cell phone with someone from Homeland Security, insisting they increase security at water-treatment plants across the country. Kat pretended to be absorbed in whatever she had up on her computer screen, but in reality, every time he looked up he caught her staring at him with eyes full of pity. Del provided the counseling.

"You really fell for her, didn't you?" he asked.

"If you consider a headfirst dive out of a 777 at thirty-five thousand feet a fall, yeah, I guess I did."

"That pretty well describes how I felt when I met Elisa."

"Yeah, but I don't have a parachute, man. A damn bug stole it. There's no soft landing in a nice, comfortable marriage at the end of this ride."

"Hmm." Del sat back, put his feet on the desk and twiddled a pencil between his fingers.

"What?"

"I've never even heard you say the *M*-word, much less use it in the same sentence as *nice,* and *comfortable.*"

"You know my mom dumped my dad before my first birthday. Left me with him."

"No, I didn't. I don't think I've ever heard you talk about your mom."

He shrugged. "I don't remember her. But my dad, he was a tough son of a bitch. I honestly believe he thought by slapping me around and making me work a full day in the oil fields at eight years old, he was preparing me for life. Making me strong. I guess he did make me strong, in a way. I learned to rely on myself, and no one else. We moved around so much, I never really let anyone else into my world. If I made friends, it just made it that much harder to leave the next time we had to pack up."

"You're not a kid anymore."

"No, but old habits are hard to break." He'd been letting those old defense mechanisms rule his life just a few days ago, when he'd decided to resign from the Rangers and leave Dallas. Instead of turning to his teammates for support, he'd closed himself off from them. "I just never learned to…connect with people. Never let anyone close enough to connect."

"I take it Macy has you rethinking this strategy?"

"Yeah. And now that I finally figured out that I need her, I'm going to lose her." He let his face fall into his hands and rubbed.

"We all know what the odds are," Del said quietly. "But no one knows for sure what's going to happen tomorrow, or the next day. No one but the big chief upstairs, and I don't mean the governor."

Clint steepled his hands in front of him and shook his head. "It's like she's given up already, Del. She's not telling her doctors what they need to do, or trying to figure out how to beat this thing. She's not trying to help herself."

Bull motioned to Del from across the room. Del stood, but rested his hand on Clint's shoulder a moment before he walked away. "Then find someone else to help her, partner."

A half hour later, Clint stood in a hallway staring— glaring, really—at a public phone booth. His partner was a genius, no doubt about it. But that didn't mean following through with his suggestion would be easy.

Macy needed someone who knew ARFIS as well as she did. Who knew Macy. She needed someone with field experience treating the disease, not just looking at it under a microscope. Only one person Clint knew fit that bill.

And yet for all that, picking up the phone and inviting David Brinker back into her life was the toughest thing Clint had ever done.

Chapter 18

The cramped room the Rangers had commandeered to work in was quiet as a morgue at midnight. None of them had left it for more than forty hours…not since Macy had learned that the terrorists planned to strike on Sunday, which was now just a sunrise away.

And not since she'd been infected with ARFIS.

Grim-faced and looking more bedraggled than Clint had seen any of them in a long while, they had regressed from touch-typing on their laptops to stabbing at the keyboards as if they could poke information out of them.

Kat set the handset of the desk phone in front of her back in its cradle and chewed on the inside of her cheek.

Del raised his head. His fingers hung suspended in midair over his computer. "What's going on in that blond head of yours, Kitty?"

She hated to be called Kitty, and Del only did it when he wanted to get a reaction out of her. The fact that she didn't seem to notice this time had Clint out of his seat and walking over to better hear what she had to say. Even Bull stopped typing and cocked his head toward them.

"I think we just got a break," Kat told them.

A ripple of...something hummed through the room.

"Elaborate," Bull ordered.

"I just got off the phone with Jackie Tucker from Josephine, Texas, outside Houston. Nice lady, by the way. Didn't even complain that I woke her up at midnight."

"Okay, I'll bite," Del said. "Who is Jackie Tucker? Besides a nice lady."

"She's a clerk with Enterprise Car Rental."

Del leaned back. His chair creaked. "I thought we didn't get any hits on our computer check of cars rented with foreign ID."

"We didn't. But I asked if they'd seen anyone that matched our descriptions—vague as they are."

"And?"

"Jackie recognized them. She said they tried to rent a car with foreign ID, but they didn't have a credit card. Tried to put a deposit down on the car with cash, but the company doesn't allow that. No plastic, no car."

"Jeez, how did we miss that?"

"Since they didn't actually get the rental, it wasn't in the database."

Bull started pacing, his long legs eating up the width of the small room in three strides. "Okay, so we know they were at—which airport in Houston?"

"Intercontinental."

"We know they were at Houston Intercontinental. Del, get on the phone and get me security video from all terminals and the rental-car counter around that time period. We might actually get our first look at these animals' faces." He scrubbed his palm over two days' worth of whiskers. "They tried to get a car and couldn't."

"We need to check the stolens." He shrugged when his three teammates all turned his way. "It's what I'd do if I needed a car and couldn't get one the regular way."

"Kat, you get on the stolen-vehicle reports. See what's missing in and around the airport that day. Clint, you can help with that."

He knew the captain was just throwing him a bone, trying to keep him busy, keep him from thinking too much. Kat was perfectly capable of running a stolen vehicle search.

"I need to go see Macy." He wanted to tell her they were making progress. Tell her to hold on.

Brinker was in with her when Clint suited up and pressed the airlock release that would admit him to her room. On seeing Clint, he got up from the chair by her bed and shuffled to the door, still looking bent and frail from his own illness. Behind him, Macy lay pale and still on the bed. A fine sheen of sweat glistened on her forehead.

"She's getting worse," Clint said.

"Her fever's up and her blood pressure's down," David whispered, as much as anyone could whisper through a respirator. "I'm starting to see some capillaries bursting under her nail beds, and hear a little fluid in her lungs."

David had arrived just six hours after Clint had called him at the Virginia VA hospital yesterday. He'd said he would have been here sooner, but he'd had to make a stop in Atlanta to pick up some interferon, a drug he thought might help Macy. Turns out he'd brought the entire CDC supply of the antiviral agent.

He'd also liberated José from the holding facility and brought him to the hospital. Something about harvesting antibodies from the monkey's plasma and mixing them with Macy's blood.

"She said none of this would work. It didn't work in Malaysia." Maybe Clint should have believed her. Maybe he should have accepted her fate with the same courage and dignity she had.

Bullshit. He wasn't accepting anything. Not until she was cold and buried. Maybe not even then.

"The effect is minimal when patients are already showing symptoms before treatment begins. But we got Macy early. And the conditions in Malaysia were deplorable. None of the patients there received the kind of supportive care she's getting."

"But it still isn't going to be enough."

David's reddened eyes filled. "Probably not, no."

"How much longer has she got?" Clint hated the way his voice croaked.

"Hard to tell. The interferon and the immune plasma are helping. They're not going to cure her, but they're slowing the progression of the disease. We're buying her time."

"How much time?" he pressed.

"Twelve, maybe eighteen hours."

Clint's gloved hand clenched. His fingers trembled, and he ignored it. His bum arm couldn't have mattered less to him at the moment.

"What about the back door that Ty mentioned? He said they had a way to kill the virus."

"My team—Macy's team—in Atlanta, and every other virologist at the CDC, are working that angle. It's theoretically possible. Just about anything is possible when you start altering an organism's genome. Much the same way a computer programmer leaves a back-door into a program, they could have programmed in an inherent vulnerability that only they would know about. It wouldn't be any harder than programming in ARFIS's lethal qualities. I supposed I'd want that safe-guard if I were a terrorist. To know that I had a way to stop it when I was ready."

Clint grunted. "Or when you'd been paid enough money. They could hold the whole world hostage with a cure to ARFIS. Can you find this back door?"

"The genetics involved are very complex. In months, or a year, maybe we could figure out what they did. But twelve hours?" He shook his head and sighed. "Every-one is trying."

"Keep trying. Buy her every second you can."

David nodded, looked from Clint to Macy. "I'll give you some privacy."

"I'd appreciate that."

He didn't know how David knew about him and Macy, but he did seem to know. Probably it was obvious just from looking at them. Watching the way they looked at each other. The doctor hadn't made an issue of it.

Lucky for him. If he had, Clint doubted he could have resisted busting the man's jaw.

Macy was drifting. Floating. But not on air or water. She felt as though she was living in a vat of clear gelatin too thick to pull into her lungs. It hurt to breathe.

She opened her eyes and saw Clint hunched over her bedside with his gloved hands holding tight to her clammy fingers. He looked like a statue. How long had he been there?

She'd been sleeping, she thought. Had she slept her life away?

He sensed her awakening. His own eyelids fluttered and those gray eyes that could see right through her swept over her face, evaluating.

"Hey, beautiful."

She coughed. "Don't make me laugh." She knew what she looked like. She'd treated a lot of women in her condition in Malaysia.

"Good news." He used tongs to gather a few ice chips from a bucket next to the bed and placed a few on her tongue. It was the closest thing to heaven she expected to experience until she arrived there in a few hours. "Brinker says you're holding your own against this thing."

"Is that another joke?"

"Totally serious."

At least he hadn't said *dead* serious.

"You've got to hold on, okay?" He squeezed her hand. "You heard Ty. The terrorists programmed in a way to kill ARFIS. Everyone at the CDC is looking for it. All your friends are trying to help you, Macy. You have to let them, by holding on."

"No. Time." Her head was going muzzy again. It was hard to concentrate.

"Then we'll get the cure from the terrorists, dammit! Wherever they are, they're bound to have some with them, just in case. We're making progress on finding them. It won't be much longer. You've just got to hold on!"

"Clint." Her throat was raw. On fire. "You have to accept—"

"I *have* accepted, Macy. I've accepted that I can't undo what's happened, as much as I want to. I've accepted that I can't take your place, as much as I want to. I've even accepted that I can't help you, at least not alone. I need Brinker, and my teammates and your teammates at the CDC to do that."

"Clint—"

"No. Listen to me. There is a difference between accepting and giving up. I have accepted. But no way am I giving up. If I'm going down, I'm going down fighting, Macy. And I want you to promise me you'll do the same."

None of the pain she was suffering because of the virus savaging her internal systems compared, at that moment, to the pain the look on his face put in her heart. The love was there, plain to see. And the sorrow. The grief.

She'd do anything to take that look away. Anything.

She took a breath and heard the fluid mixing with the air in her lungs. "It's hard."

"I know it is." He leaned over so that his face shield was just inches from her nose. "But people survive ARFIS, just like they survive other viruses like HIV and Lassa Fever and Ebola."

She wanted to laugh, but didn't have enough air. "What do you know about Ebola?"

"I've been surfing the Net."

She saw a flicker of light across the wall, and realized someone had entered the observation room. Managing to turn her head a fraction of an inch, she saw Clint's captain behind the glass.

He switched on the intercom between the rooms. "Clint, we have to go."

She tightened her grip on his hand. *No.* Not yet.

"See?" Clint said, and produced another fake smile. "We're closing in on the terrorists. He wouldn't pull me out of here for any other reason."

"Stay," she croaked.

He lifted her hand to his face shield as if he could bring it all the way to his lips and kiss her knuckles. "I want to. You know I do. But I have to go. I have to keep fighting, for both of us."

And she knew he was right. He would keep fighting long after she was able.

He was her last defense.

He pulled something out of the pouch at the waist of his suit and put it in her hand. It was cool and smooth. Metallic, like his eyes.

"What is it?" she asked. She couldn't lift her head to look.

He lifted her hand, with whatever it was still in it, so she could see.

"Your badge?"

He curved her fingers over the silver circle and star so that it pressed into her palm. "I want you to hold on to it for me. Don't lose it. I'm going to need it back soon."

"But—" Involuntarily, her bleary gaze landed on his bad shoulder.

"I told you, I'm not giving up. On anything. I'm going to find a way to keep doing what I do whether I can hold a gun or not. But I need you to help me. I need you there with me. I love you, Macy. I love you."

Then he backed away from the bed and was gone before Macy could gather the strength to tell him she loved him, too. Yet even when he was gone, Macy couldn't help feeling as if he were still there. He'd left her more than his badge.

He'd left her his heart.

She closed her hand over it and held on tight.

"What've you got?" Clint strode down the hall from the decon room with Bull at his side, though every cell in his body screamed for him to go back. To stay with her.

He was very much afraid he might never see her again.

"Three stolen cars around Houston Intercontinental Airport around the time our boys were there. A red Corvette."

Clint jerked his head to the side. "Too flashy. Our guys would want to keep a low profile. And there are four of them. They wouldn't fit in a 'Vette."

"Second car is a beat-up old truck with the tailpipe wired on. I'm thinking they'd want something more reliable. Wouldn't want to chance breaking down."

"I'm with you." Though at least half of him was still in the room down the hall, with Macy.

"Third vehicle is a white Chevy van. Late model. No windows, like a business van."

Clint stopped just outside the door to the Ranger's room. "That's it. Now all we have to do is find it."

"We already have. A Dallas PD beat cop saw it parked outside Texas Stadium an hour ago and ran the plates. They were just getting ready to send out a tow when I put a hold on it and told them to back off."

"Texas Stadium? Do the Cowboys have a home game tomorrow?"

Bull nodded tightly.

"Was there any sign of our suspects?"

"The officer said the place looked secure, but he didn't go inside. He figured the van had been abandoned."

Clint chewed on that. "Maybe he scared them off."

"Or maybe they'd already gone."

"Or maybe they were still inside, working, and had no idea there was a cop on their doorstep. How long ago was this?"

"An hour."

"We can be there in a less than two, better if we fly."

"Chopper's already on the way."

Bull held the door while Del and Kat poured through, carrying their gear. Clint turned to follow his teammates, but Bull held him back with a hand on his arm. "By the way, what was all that about you finding a way to do what you do, even if you can't hold a gun?"

Clint's chest constricted. He could lie, or he could dodge the question. But if Macy could tackle ARFIS without complaint, he could face up to a little nerve damage. He just didn't want to delay getting to the terrorists—and a possible cure for Macy—a second longer.

He pulled out of Bull's grasp. "Come on. I'll explain on the way."

Chapter 19

Brinker leaned over Macy's bed and wondered if she could still see him. Still hear him. He had to go on as if she could.

"Macy, I'm going to intubate you now to help you breathe."

"No." Her voice sounded as though she'd swallowed glass, but he was glad to hear it no matter how it sounded. "Have you…heard from him?"

David didn't have to ask who "him" was. He'd seen the way she looked at her Ranger. She'd never looked at him that way.

And, he had to admit, he'd never looked at her that way, either. In his own way, he'd loved her. But he'd loved his science more. It wasn't until he thought he was losing her that he'd become desperate to keep her. He'd have to live with what he'd done as a result for the rest of his life, and still it would never be punishment enough.

He should be the one with ARFIS, the one dying. Not her.

Not her.

If she died, if anyone else died because of him, he wasn't sure his life would be worth living.

"No word yet, honey, but I'm sure they'll all be back soon. They had a good lead. They'll come back and they'll bring the cure."

"Tell him, David," she whispered hoarsely.

"Tell him what?"

"Tell him to be strong. Don't give up."

"I'll tell him, honey. I know he'd tell you the same thing if he were here right now."

"Tell him I know he'll find a way to keep doing what he does." She swallowed painfully. "Tell him I love him."

"He knows, honey." He stroked damp curls back from her forehead. He could feel her fever even through two pairs of gloves. "He knows."

As her eyes closed again, he curled her fingers around the silver circle and star in her limp palm, then picked up the synthetic hose that would hold her airway open as her body's organs began to shut down, one by one.

"What the hell is taking so long?"

A block away from the football stadium, Clint marched back and forth outside the mobile command post.

"You know the drill," Del said calmly beside him, waiting in full tactical gear—a reminder to Clint that his fate and Macy's was out of his hands now. Thanks to his undependable arm, he would be stuck in the command post handling radio traffic while his friends entered the stadium.

He guessed it was better than being left out of the operation altogether. The Rangers had taken the news pretty well. Been sympathetic without making a big emotional scene. Thank God for that. His emotions were in enough of a turmoil already today. He just wanted to get this over with. Get back to Macy.

"This is a big place," Del continued. "We had to call in SWAT teams from five suburbs to cover it. Dallas Fire Department just now got here with the hazmat gear. The captain had to study blueprints of the structure, come up with a plan. Everybody has to be briefed. It takes time."

"It's been over an hour."

"And it'll probably be another before we go."

And another couple of hours to get the cure back to Houston. If they found a cure.

Too long. It was taking too long. Assuming Macy was still alive when they got back. Even if she was, it might be too late. If her internal organs were too badly damaged, she couldn't survive even if they did manage to kill the virus in her system.

He checked his watch. "If they're here, they've been in there almost all night."

"I imagine it's delicate work tapping into the water lines without setting off any alarms or causing a flood.

And they've got to have some kind of complicated setup to keep the virus alive in a contained environment until they're ready to release it into the water. Otherwise the virus would all be dead before people arrived for the game tomorrow. Plus they'd probably want to insert the virus at multiple points in the system, to catch as many people as they can, and as a failsafe. That's all gotta take time."

Del was right. But what if they weren't in there? What if they were long gone, their cure with them?

He and the other officers here would have saved the city, maybe the country, from a major catastrophe, he told himself.

But Macy would still die.

"So how come you didn't tell me about your arm?" Del said, watching him pace from his position propped against the van. Trying to distract Clint? Or honestly hurt that he hadn't leaned on him? He wasn't sure.

"We're supposed to be partners," Del said. "Not to mention it was my wife you were trying to save when you got shot. Makes me kind of responsible, you know?"

No distraction. Del was stinging. And more than a little pissed off underneath that veneer of calm.

"It was nobody's fault but my own I got shot. And I wanted to say something to you, to all of you. I just…couldn't bring myself to do it."

"You mean you were in denial."

"That, too."

Del heaved out a deep breath and rolled his shoulders. Clint felt for him. His partner had been standing around in fifty pounds of Kevlar for an hour. Plus he had the added burden of the gas mask slung over his shoulder, and the weight of the danger he was about to walk into squarely on his shoulders. It wore on a man.

"I still feel responsible," he muttered.

"You think you owe me? Now's the perfect time to pay the debt. You make sure nothing goes wrong in there. Take those guys down and find that cure, if they've got one."

Before Del could respond, the door of the command center swung open. Bull Matheson stuck his head out. "Green light. Get ready."

Time accelerated. Seconds that seemed to drag by just moments ago now flew as men in heavy armor scrambled to get in position.

Bull Matheson gathered his team and looked at Clint. "You keep track of the other teams. Keep us out of the cross fire if it gets dicey in there."

"Will do."

"Everybody check your masks. Make sure your gloves don't have any tears. Hazmat showers will be waiting when we come out, just in case." He turned his attention to Kat. "And you stay with me. No matter what."

Her "will do" was notably absent. Bull had been sitting on her like a hen on a chick since she'd joined the team. It looked like she was starting to resent it. Bull didn't seem to notice, though, as he looked back to Clint. "If there's anything in there that can help the doctor, we'll find it."

A lump the size of San Antonio lodged in Clint's throat. These were his friends, dressed out like knights in armor and ready to put their lives on the line to save the damsel in distress.

And a few hundred thousand other lives, he reminded himself. Every kid who washed his hands in the bathroom or person who took a drink from the public fountain at tomorrow's game was at risk. Then they'd take ARFIS home to their friends and families, who would spread it to their coworkers when they went back to work Monday morning, and on and on.

Where would it stop? Would it stop at all, or were they looking at a biological Armegeddon?

He couldn't say anything to his team, his partners, so he just nodded.

Moments later he sat behind a console with dozens of switches and buttons, a headset pulled tightly down over his ears and microphone in front of his mouth.

"All teams, on my mark." He blew out his breath, said a short prayer. "Go."

Keeping track of the three entry teams and the resources deployed outside for containment should anyone try to bolt required every bit of Clint's attention for the next ten minutes, and still he had a sense of a clock in the back of his mind, the hands sweeping around, ticking away the seconds of Macy's life.

"Control, this is red team."

"Control. Go, red team."

"We've reached the boiler room. No sign of targets."

He heard Kat's voice, high-pitched as always when her adrenaline was flowing. "I'm going to check the water lines."

"No, wait for me."

"There's no one here, Cap—"

What Del heard next was hard to interpret. Running feet. Labored breathing. Muttered curses. The oomph of one body slamming into another.

The explosion that came next required no interpretation.

"All teams, hold position! Red team leader? Red team leader? Status."

Only static answered him.

"Control, blue team leader. We're close. We'll go."

"No." His stomach twisted, wanting to send help, send eyes to tell him what was happening, but he couldn't put more officers in danger. "Hold your position."

"Red team. Reply. Red team."

Relief washed over him when he heard someone's harsh breathing come on the line. "Control, the place is booby-trapped." Del. What about the others? "Explosive devices deployed. Red team leader is down. Repeat, red team leader is down."

"Can you get him out?"

"The way we came in. Have medics meet us at the exit," Del replied grimly. "It's bad, Clint. Real bad."

An hour and a half later, Del stepped out of the mobile command center. Kat crouched by a wheel well, still in her body armor, with her face in her hands. Del waited for him at the bottom of the stairs.

"She feels responsible."

"He told her to stay with him."

"Any of us would have done the same thing, checked

out the water lines. Hell, I was headed over there my-self. She just got there first."

"Bull saw the device?"

Del nodded. "Practically threw her out of the way about a half second before it blew. Took the full force of it himself. Any word from the hospital?"

"No. It could be awhile. I'm sure he's still in E.R." At least he hoped the captain was in E.R, and not the morgue. He'd seen the injuries. Del had been right. It was bad. Real bad. "I gave them my cell phone number and asked them to call as soon as they knew anything."

"So that's it?" Del asked. "It's over?"

"Blue team and green teams both found virus canis-ters with material to sustain live virus tapped into the water lines, along with what the clean-up crew found at your location. All three sites were booby-trapped. But there was no sign of the targets."

Del swore. "I'm sorry."

Clint was sorry, too. His chest felt cold and dead with sorry, despite the lives they'd saved.

"They were probably gone long before we got here. Must have seen the first cop who stopped to check out the van, decided they could do without it and hoofed it in the opposite direction."

"Maybe someone saw them on the road. It's not like there's anything else real close, anywhere they could have gone."

Clint heard him, but his mind was somewhere else. "Have they towed the van yet?"

"No. Hazmat crew wants to have a look first, make sure there's no more virus in it."

Clint was jogging across the parking lot before Del finished the sentence. He blew by the uniformed officers securing the van and stopped by the driver's door, cupping his hands to peer in the windows. Del was right behind him.

"What are you doing? Hey, you don't even have hazmat gear on."

"The hell with it." He tried the door handle. Locked. He broke the driver's side window with the butt of his gun. At least the damn thing still served some purpose.

"Hope that these guys didn't carry all their gear into the stadium with them."

He crawled across the driver's seat, checking the glove compartment and center console. Del opened the side door and checked the cargo area. "Nothing."

"Nothing here, either." Then Clint bent over, and hissed in a breath.

Under the passenger seat was an insulated lunch bag, zippered closed. He pulled it out gently, ran the tab back to open it, and pulled out a plastic baggie with four small, brown vials inside.

Del leaned over the passenger seat from the back. "Is it virus, or cure?"

"I don't know," Clint said. "But I know someone who will."

Macy gradually became aware of a bright light in front of her. It pulled at her consciousness. It called to her. She wanted to go to the light. Down deep in her soul she needed to go to the light, but she was afraid. Afraid this was *the* light. The eternal light. The light of the hereafter.

Isn't that what all those near-death stories described? A bright light that called to them, promised them warmth and comfort beyond words?

Innumerable aches and pains began to make themselves known to Macy. She'd never been flattened by a truck, but this had to be what it felt like. Her head throbbed. Her throat felt raw. Her arms and legs felt like lumps of clay attached to her torso.

She tried to drift back, back to the dark where she'd been—how long? It was cold there, and lonely, but at least there was no pain. No light tempting her to give up her life.

Clint had asked her to fight, and for him, and because she didn't want to die before she had a chance to tell him she loved him, she had fought. She'd fought with every ounce of her will and her strength. But both those were gone now, and no matter how hard she tried to crawl back to the darkness, the light called her. It called her with such insistence that she couldn't hold on any longer.

Choking back a sob, she let go. She floated toward the light. The bright rays warmed and filled her, took away some of the pain, and she stopped fighting. She opened her eyes to face the light, and what lay on the other side.

Gradually a figure took shape in the light. A dark silhouette, tall and lanky. The hazy edges of the light sharpened until she realized it wasn't a light at all, or at least not that light, but a window with the sun shining brightly through it.

In front of the glass stood her Ranger, calling her name.

Was he really here—wherever here was—or was she having some sort of out-of-body experience?

"Clint?" Her throat felt as if someone had scrubbed it with a wire brush.

He jammed his fingertips into the pockets of his jeans and strode toward her. She still couldn't see much of him. The light behind him was too strong. It hid his face and made her eyes water.

"Hey, beautiful," he said.

She snuffled. Blinked. "You came back."

"I told you I would."

"Need— Need to tell you—" She couldn't get the rest out. She needed to take a breath first. Several breaths.

He stopped beside her. "Tell me what?"

"G-goodbye." Her tears welled over her eyelids to leave warm trails down her cheeks. "And I love you. Didn't— Didn't get to tell you. Before."

"I'll take the 'I love you,' part. But this isn't good-bye. More like hello again." He propped one hip on the edge of her bed and used his thumbs to wipe away her tears.

For the first time, she realized he wasn't wearing any protective gear. Fear exploded inside her like an over-filled water balloon. She tried to scrabble back, away from him, but she was so weak all she managed was to thrash against the sheets. "No! Clint, don't touch me. Mask. You need a mask! Please—"

Horror strangled the rest of what she wanted to say.

"Shhh. It's all right." He stilled her with his big hands on her shaking shoulders, then framed her face. "It's okay. The virus is all gone. It's been out of your system for days."

ARFIS, gone? While she tried to comprehend what he was saying, he let her go, straightened up and the impenetrable shield he usually wore over his expression fell away. He smiled.

Clint, smiling?

He had a beautiful smile. White and straight and strong.

"You still gave us a scare. The virus had done quite a number on your systems. It took a few days to stabilize you, but you're going to be fine."

"B-but…how?"

He dipped a finger under the neck of her hospital gown, lifted a thin chain. On the end of it dangled the silver star and circle. "Texas Rangers always get their man." His smile broadened. "Even the microscopic ones."

Epilogue

It was a perfect night in heaven.

The last few leaves of fall clung to the trees under a silver-dollar moon. The surface of Lake Farrell, the best fishing hole in southeast Texas, or so Clint told her, rippled like black velvet. And the air, sharp with the scent of pine, was clean enough to scrub the last remnants of illness out of a woman's lungs with each breath.

Macy stood in the doorway of Clint's cabin, with José chattering happily in her arms and picking at her hair. After the monkey had helped save her life, she could hardly have abandoned the poor thing. He'd adjusted amazingly quickly to life as a pet. He was already spoiled rotten.

José lifted one simian hand and pointed toward the lake, his voice raising from chatter to full squawk.

"Yes, I see him."

Out on the pier, her husband placed beer bottles in a neat row and then headed back to shore.

They'd been married by the hospital chaplain as soon as she was strong enough to sit up. He didn't want to miss out on a single day living with her as his wife, Clint had claimed. He'd let her hold on to his badge until he replaced it with a ring.

"Watch this," he said as he stepped back on the porch.

Then he sat down in the creaky old grapevine chair and frowned at her bare feet on the cold planks. Nearly a month had passed since she'd woken in the hospital, weak and disoriented, and he still worried about her.

He motioned her over with his fingers and pulled her into his lap, tucking the quilt she had slung over her shoulders carefully over every exposed bit of skin before lifting his gun.

In his left hand.

"Plug your ears," he said.

She did, and turned her face into his shoulder to protect her eyes. She knew what was coming. He'd started training himself to shoot with his non-dominant hand over a month ago. The question was, was it working?

Clint fired three rounds, and she raised her head to see, almost afraid to look. His early efforts had met with frustration, but he'd been practicing religiously. She knew how important it was to him.

She smiled at the empty pier railing. "Three out of three? Not bad."

His face turned serious. "Not good enough, though. I got a call from Austin today."

She tensed. "Ranger headquarters?" He'd been waiting for them to decide his fate, she knew.

He nodded. "The powers that be have reviewed the test results from the neurologist. They're not going to let me back in the field, even if I can qualify on the gun range with my left hand."

Her heart swelled into her throat. She stroked his cheek with her fingertips, and he snugged her closer to him. "I'm sorry, Clint."

"Don't be. They're not going to let me in the field, and I'll miss that. But they had another proposal."

She waited for him to explain, sensing the change in direction was something he was still working through.

"After our brush with disaster, it seems the governor is interested in starting up a new task force. An anti-terrorism group aimed specifically at protecting Texas and Texans from terrorism. It would be state level, but would coordinate with the federal agencies like Homeland Security and the FBI. He was thinking the Rangers would be the perfect group to run it."

"They asked you to be on this team?" She wasn't sure how she felt about that, honestly. The four men who had sabotaged Texas Stadium had been caught in Chicago two days later, trying to buy train tickets to Canada. It turned out they'd been from two separate hate groups—one Middle Eastern and one from the disease, poverty and famine-ravaged Sudan—who had joined forces, a terrifying trend in itself.

The drug that had saved her life had already been analyzed and duplicated in Atlanta. The project had been David's last for the CDC. He'd known going in that they would terminate him afterward. At least they'd given him a chance to redeem himself somewhat for the damage he felt responsible for. He'd worked tirelessly and cracked the cure in record time.

The results of his new drug in Malaysia were very positive. He was there now, working without compensation to treat those still recovering from the disease.

The threat of anyone using ARFIS as a biological weapon had been nullified. But how many more plots to kill or maim were being cooked up out there? How many more times would Clint have to put his life on the line to stop them?

On the other hand, being a Ranger wasn't just what he did. It was part of who he was, and she loved him. All of him.

She would learn to deal with it.

"You won't have to give up your badge?" she asked.

"Not give it up. Just trade it in." He lifted his quicksilver gaze to hers. "For one that says captain on it."

Joy bloomed inside her. "You're getting a promotion?"

He nodded. "They didn't just ask me to be on the task force. They asked me to lead it."

She threw her arms around his neck and hugged him tight. "Congratulations, Captain."

"I'm not sure how it's going to work out. It'll mean riding a desk a lot, but I guess I'll adjust. I can always call Bull for advice."

She pulled back, sobered. "How is he?"

"Regaining his strength, slowly."

"Still no word from Kat?"

The pretty blond Ranger had taken off without a word as soon as Captain Matheson had come out of emergency surgery, Macy had been told. No one had heard from her since.

Clint shook his head. "Del's been trying to track her down, but with the baby due any day, he's had to stick close to home."

"She blames herself."

"That's why it's so important we find her. I hate to think of her out there alone. She needs some help dealing with it."

"You'll find her." She hoped it was true.

"Yeah." Clint pulled the quilt tighter around her. "You cold?"

"No, it's a beautiful night."

He kissed her gently, sweetly, gradually taking her deeper, arousal rolling in between them like the tide. "Could be a beautiful night inside too. In that big, warm bed in there."

"Could be."

She smiled against his lips as he lifted her, carried her over the threshold.

It was a perfect night in heaven, indeed.

* * * * *

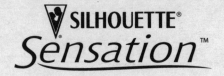

▼ SILHOUETTE®
Sensation™

AWAKEN TO DANGER
by Catherine Mann

Wingmen Warriors

Nikki Price's world comes crashing down when she wakes up next to a dead body. And the nightmare continues as the man who broke her heart, Squadron Commander Carson Hunt, is sent to investigate. Carson's certain Nikki's in danger and vows to protect her. But will she be able to trust him with her life...and her heart?

LIVING ON THE EDGE
by Susan Mallery

Bodyguard Tanner Keane expected his assignment to rescue a kidnapped heiress to be straightforward. And yet Madison Hilliard wasn't at all what he expected. As passion sparked between them, would their combustible attraction stand in the way of bringing down a deadly enemy?

BREAKING ALL THE RULES
by Susan Vaughan

Bad-boy government officer Simon Byrne avoided relationships. By-the-book tech officer Janna Harris wasn't the type to get involved, either. Pairing these two ex-lovers in a high-risk investigation will test their boundaries...and the passion that could threaten their lives.

On sale from 20th October 2006

*Available at WHSmith, Tesco, ASDA, Borders, Eason,
Sainsbury's and most bookshops*

www.silhouette.co.uk

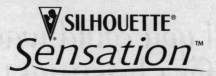

SILHOUETTE®
Sensation™

1006/18b

LOOK-ALIKE by Meredith Fletcher
Bombshell—Athena Force

Spy sisters Elle and Sam must deal with their conflicting loyalties—Sam to the US, Elle to Russia—as they search for the truth about their parents' deaths. But Elle must also contend with her undeniable attraction to a man who at best is an enigma and at worst a criminal…

BLUE JEANS AND A BADGE
by Nina Bruhns

Bounty hunter Luce Montgomery and chief of police Phillip O'Donnaugh were on the prowl for a fugitive. As the stakes rose, so did their mutual attraction. Phillip was desperate to break through the wall between them but Luce was still reeling from revelations about her past that even blue jeans and a badge might not cure…

MS LONGSHOT by Sylvie Kurtz
Bombshell—The IT Girls

Top show horses were dying in suspicious circumstances, so the Gotham Rose spies called on socialite Alexa Cheltingham to go undercover as a grubby groom. Her riches-to-rags transition wasn't easy, but she had to protect the mayor's show-jumping daughter, hunt for the horse killer, even dodge a murder rap. And all while resist her chief suspect's undeniable charms…

On sale from 20th October 2006

Available at WHSmith, Tesco, ASDA, Borders, Eason, Sainsbury's and most bookshops

www.silhouette.co.uk

1106/XMAS TITLES a

All you could want for Christmas!

Meet handsome and seductive men under the mistletoe, escape to the world of Regency romance or simply relax by the fire with a heartwarming tale by one of our bestselling authors. These special stories will fill your holiday with Christmas sparkle!

On sale 6th October 2006

On sale 20th October 2006

On sale
3rd November
2006

1106/XMAS TITLES b

DIANA PALMER
JOAN JOHNSTON

Under the
Mistletoe

DEBBIE
MACOMBER

There's Something
About Christmas

A Lover for
Christmas

WANTED: A FAMILY FOR
CHRISTMAS

Linda Warren Mollie Molay

Yuletide
Weddings

On sale 17th November 2006

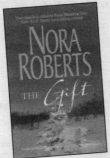

NORA
ROBERTS

The Gift

On sale
1st December
2006

Available at
WHSmith, Asda,
Tesco and all
good bookshops

www.millsandboon.co.uk

M&B

4 FREE

BOOKS AND A SURPRISE GIFT!

We would like to take this opportunity to thank you for reading this Silhouette® book by offering you the chance to take FOUR more specially selected titles from the Sensation™ series absolutely FREE! We're also making this offer to introduce you to the benefits of the Mills & Boon® Reader Service™—

- ★ **FREE home delivery**
- ★ **FREE gifts and competitions**
- ★ **FREE monthly Newsletter**
- ★ **Exclusive Reader Service offers**
- ★ **Books available before they're in the shops**

Accepting these FREE books and gift places you under no obligation to buy, you may cancel at any time, even after receiving your free shipment. Simply complete your details below and return the entire page to the address below. You don't even need a stamp!

YES! Please send me 4 free Sensation books and a surprise gift. I understand that unless you hear from me, I will receive 6 superb new titles every month for just £3.10 each, postage and packing free. I am under no obligation to purchase any books and may cancel my subscription at any time. The free books and gift will be mine to keep in any case.

S6ZED

Ms/Mrs/Miss/Mr ....Initials ....

BLOCK CAPITALS PLEASE

Surname ....

Address ....

....

....Postcode..................................

Send this whole page to:
UK: FREEPOST CN81, Croydon, CR9 3WZ

Offer valid in UK only and is not available to current Mills & Boon® Reader Service™ subscribers to this series. Overseas and Eire please write for details. We reserve the right to refuse an application and applicants must be aged 18 years or over. Only one application per household. Terms and prices subject to change without notice. Offer expires 31st January 2007. As a result of this application, you may receive offers from Harlequin Mills & Boon and other carefully selected companies. If you would prefer not to share in this opportunity please write to The Data Manager, PO Box 676, Richmond, TW9 1WU.

Silhouette® is a registered trademark and under licence.
Sensation™ is being used as a trademark. The Mills & Boon® Reader Service™ is being used as a trademark.